ISLAND HOUSE

BRU BAKER

Dreamspinner Press

Published by
Dreamspinner Press
5032 Capital Circle SW
Suite 2, PMB# 279
Tallahassee, FL 32305-7886
USA
http://www.dreamspinnerpress.com/

Island House
© 2013 Bru Baker.

Cover Art
© 2013 L.C. Chase.
http://www.lcchase.com
Cover content is for illustrative purposes only and any person depicted on the cover is a model.

ISBN: 978-1-62798-314-3
Digital ISBN: 13978-1-62798-315-0

Printed in the United States of America
First Edition
November 2013

I am blessed to have supportive friends who keep me on track and are always available for plot emergencies and last-minute editing. Shannon and Betsy, your help was instrumental! And thanks to my husband, Ross, who herds the kids out of the house whenever he can so I can write in peace. Love you!

ONE

NIALL AHERN straightened his cuff links, pursing his lips over the formality of his outfit. He'd last worn this suit at his niece's baptism a few months after her birth, and Camille would be eight that fall. But his discomfort stemmed more from the fact it was August in the British Virgin Islands, not the age of the suit. It still fit perfectly, the brushed wool trousers skimming over his trim waist and toned thighs and the sleeves just kissing his wrists, cuff links appropriately visible. But Camille's baptism had been in November, not to mention it had also been in cool, overcast London instead of the oppressively hot island paradise he was currently wearing it in.

"Must be waitin' on someone important, all turned out like you iz." Niall whirled around, rolling his eyes when he saw the tall dark-skinned man leaning against a luggage trolley. The fabric of his garishly colored tie-dyed shirt stretched across his belly, its mishmash of colors standing out starkly against the beige walls of the small airport terminal.

"Not that I'm going to tell you how to run your business, because God knows I certainly can't give tips on success, but do you have to put on such a ridiculous accent when the tourists aren't here, Jacks?"

The older man straightened and grinned, revealing perfect teeth. It made a remarkable difference, his belly all but disappearing as he stood at his full height.

"It's what customers expect," Jacks said with a shrug. "Bettina did a study on it when she took a marketing class up at the college. She had us switch back and forth, using the accent for a week and then not for a week. She had a spreadsheet and everything. Customers tipped 30 percent more when we sounded like backwater Rastas."

Niall shook his head, fidgeting with his cuff links again. He was absolutely baking in the heavy suit, but he'd worn it because he needed to impress the client, who was due any minute. The small real estate office Niall had opened on the island two years earlier was floundering. He sorely needed the commission that would come from brokering a multimillion-dollar deal. So he'd gone with the suit and given himself the best pep talk he could before heading out, trying to ignore the fact that the future of his business rested squarely in the infamously picky tech mogul Ethan Bettencourt's hands.

"Think it would work for me?" he asked, giving Jacks his most charming smile. The nerves that had been churning in his stomach eased a bit as Jacks threw back his head and laughed, the familiar sound putting Niall more at ease than he'd been all morning.

"I don't think so, mon," he drawled. "You're missing the key characteristic."

Niall grinned, narrowing his eyes and inspecting Jacks carefully.

"Actually being Jamaican? You're missing it too."

"Niall, I hate to be the one to break it to you, but—" Whatever Jacks was about to say was lost as another voice interrupted them, catching Niall off guard, since his back had been to the door.

"You're Ahern?"

The voice belonged to a tall, dark-haired man who would have been handsome save for the stubble covering his face. The rugged two-day growth transformed his slightly sharp features into something dangerous, and paired with his slight tan and blue eyes, the end result was nothing short of breathtakingly gorgeous. Were it not for the faded button-down and pair of tattered Dockers the man was wearing, Niall would have sworn he was an 18th century pirate somehow transported to the modern day.

Niall didn't realize he'd been staring, until Jacks cleared his throat and stepped forward, hand outstretched to welcome the visitor. Niall swallowed, his already heat-flushed cheeks burning with the beginnings of a blush. He hadn't reacted to a man like this since—well, since ever. Niall's only serious relationship had been with a man he'd known since childhood, and it definitely hadn't started with a spark of lust like this. He felt a familiar pang of guilt at the thought of finding a man other than Nolan attractive, though Nolan had been gone for years.

"Sorry?" Niall asked when it became clear the would-be pirate was talking to him again.

"I asked if you were Niall Ahern," the man said, blue eyes narrowed slightly as he studied Niall. "He said he'd be here to pick me up—"

"Mr. Bettencourt!" Niall felt his stomach drop. Ethan Bettencourt was one of the world's most sought-after software developers and technology consultants. He wore Armani suits and custom-made Italian shoes, not ancient Dockers and flip-flops. But as Niall stared at him, he could see the full lips and aquiline nose that had made Ethan fodder for gossip magazines across the world. It was definitely him.

"I'm so sorry, sir," Niall said, rushing forward. He wasn't sure if he should shake his hand or offer to take his luggage, and as a result he did neither, hand raised awkwardly in front of him as his mind tried to catch up and figure out what to do.

Bettencourt solved Niall's dilemma by shifting his bag to his other hand and reaching out to take Niall's half-raised hand. "Call me Ethan."

The contact had Niall cringing inside, the cool skin of Ethan's hand making him even more aware of his own sweaty palm.

"Of course," Niall said, cursing himself for being so flustered. He'd never had this problem before when greeting important clients. Of course, he'd never had an important client who was as gorgeous as Ethan, nor one who could keep Niall's business afloat for another year with a single transaction.

"Welcome to the islan', Ethan," Jacks said, sliding back into his put-on accent and into an easy conversation with Ethan about his flight and the weather forecast for the next few days. It bought Niall enough time to marshal his thoughts, and he made a mental note to buy Jacks a beer the next time he saw him at The Cab, the tiny bar where most of the locals gathered to get away from tourists.

"My car is just outside," Niall said, reaching out with more grace this time to take Ethan's bag. Ethan let him, his full lips quirking into a small smile that had Niall's heart racing again. "I thought you might like a chance to settle in at the hotel. If you like, I can leave you with some of the information on the listings we'll be looking at tomorrow."

Ethan's eyes narrowed slightly, and he dug in his pocket, pulling out a Blackberry that looked like it had been through a war zone. The screen was scuffed and the back was covered with scrapes and deep scratches. It was more suited to a rock climber or beach bum than a man who'd made his fortune in technology. Before Niall could say anything, Ethan had dialed and was pressing the phone against his ear, his tanned knuckles skimming his jaw.

"Explain to me why Mr. Ahern has no idea I'm staying with him for the duration of my trip to Tortola," he barked into the phone without preamble, startling Niall with both the tone of his voice and the unexpected information.

Niall's brow creased, his brain registering Ethan's words as the other man lapsed into silence, apparently listening to whoever was on the other end of the phone. He'd had his office manager, Keandra, handle all the arrangements for Ethan's visit. Niall had assumed she'd gotten Ethan a suite at Frenchman's Lookout. It was standard operating procedure with their high-end clients, even though accommodations at the pricey resort cost Niall more than double his monthly mortgage on his boat and the office combined. The hotel gave him a bit of a discount, since he was a local, but still, it was a shock every time the bill came. Regardless, it was worth it. Even if he spent upward of $10,000 wining and dining a single client for a week.

"… absolutely not. I'll fly back if that's the case."

Niall's head flicked up at the finality in Ethan's tone. He was obviously not happy with whatever the person on the other end of the battered cell phone was telling him. Niall swallowed, mentally inventorying the state of his house. He hadn't been home in weeks, as per his usual September routine. It was the one month out of the year Niall decamped to his boat and lived on it full-time. His quick trip home to change into the suit he was wearing had been the first time he'd been in the bungalow since the beginning of the month. Niall made a quick mental study of the rooms, trying to picture whether he'd seen laundry strewn around the bathroom or plates cluttering the kitchen. He didn't think there had been.

Niall wondered if he should pull out his own phone and call Keandra, but it was her afternoon off. He hated to bother her when she was out with her son. Between her job as Niall's office manager and working second shift at The Cab, she didn't have much time with Sebastian. He was brushing the top of his pocket to delve inside for his cell when Ethan made a disgusted noise and stabbed at a button on his phone, glaring at it for good measure before tossing it haphazardly on top of the suitcase he'd set on the terminal floor. No mystery to why it was so banged up, then, Niall thought absently as Ethan swung his black gaze over to focus on him.

"Apparently there has been a miscommunication." Ethan ground his teeth together, the motion making the tendons in his neck stand out in a way Niall knew should have been off-putting but wasn't. "Susannah somehow overlooked the arrangements your secretary sent her along with the appointment confirmation."

Niall wondered if Susannah would still have a job when her boss returned to the mainland; Ethan was infamous for his hair-trigger temper and his exacting standards. Niall had done a fair bit of research on Ethan when he'd taken him on as a client, and one thing that had come up time and again was Ethan's penchant for dramatics.

Niall felt for the secretary. It couldn't be easy to work for someone as demanding as Ethan Bettencourt. He was beginning to find that out firsthand, and he'd only been in his employ for several minutes.

"I only have thirty-six hours to find a home, Ahern, and I don't intend to waste any of them lounging poolside at whatever passes for a resort here," Ethan snapped. Niall stiffened his spine at the insult. Tortola was the gem of the British Virgin Islands, a place he and Nolan had handpicked out of dozens of potential islands when they'd been looking for a place to start a business. He opened his mouth to respond, but Ethan was off and running again before Niall could form any words. "I'll be staying with you. If you have a problem with that, I'll find someone else to work with."

Niall's lips flattened at the threat. There were plenty of other firms here Ethan could give his business to; Niall knew that all too well. His tiny independent real estate firm hardly caught any of the multimillion-dollar action, and the thought of losing such a big client made his skin turn clammy under the weight of his heavy suit. He was sure Ethan knew he couldn't afford to lose the commission; in fact, he wouldn't put it past him to have picked Niall's firm simply because he knew Niall's desperation would make him agree to just about anything.

"You'd be much more comfortable at a hotel." Niall ground the words out, forcing himself to smile.

6

Ethan studied him for a second before patting his pockets in search of his phone. Niall was about to point it out on his suitcase when Ethan pulled a slimmer, sleeker phone out of his shirt pocket. It was much more in line with what Niall had expected a man like Ethan to carry.

"Change in plans." Just like before, Ethan didn't pause for the person on the other end to get a greeting in. "Refuel the plane and have it ready for me in ten minutes."

Niall's eyes widened and he stepped forward slightly, panicked. "I—"

"Joe? Never mind."

Niall watched Ethan end the call, Ethan's full lips twisted into a smirk. It made Niall wonder if Ethan really would have left. The calculating gleam in the other man's eyes made him pretty certain it hadn't been an empty threat.

"You be needin' a car, Mr. Niall?" Jacks's voice took Niall off guard, and he shook his head slightly. He'd driven to the airport, as he was sure Jacks well knew. The parking lot wasn't very big, and Jacks would have seen the familiar battered Mercedes when he parked his cab.

"No, Jacks. We'll be fine," Niall said. His brain felt woolly and like it was trying to catch up. He'd been in a fog ever since Ethan had stepped into the terminal, and he needed to shake it off.

"Storm's comin'," Jacks said, picking up Ethan's bag and walking toward the exit as if Niall hadn't spoken. For a second, he wondered if he hadn't actually said the words out loud, but then Ethan turned toward him and arched an eyebrow.

"Your car?"

"Right." Niall jogged a few paces to catch up with Ethan and Jacks, the wind outside drawing his attention for the first time. It had kicked up considerably since he'd arrived at the airport. The tall palms were thrashing from side to side and the sky was an ominous shade of dark gray.

"Didn't think Sookie was supposed to make landfall here," Niall said, squinting at the clouds that seemed to be hovering unusually low.

"That's Thalia." Ethan shrugged when both Jacks and Niall looked surprised to hear him weigh in. "Sookie fell apart, but Thalia was right behind it. Looks like we won't get so lucky with her."

God, he hoped the storm didn't actually hit, Niall thought sourly as he opened the trunk for Jacks. That's all he needed, to be stuck in a tiny bungalow with his jackass of a client during a tropical storm.

TWO

CONSIDERING THEY hadn't gotten started until midafternoon, Niall managed to show Ethan an astounding number of properties before dusk set in, muddying the breathtakingly expensive views. They'd seen several hillside homes with lavish terraced decks, all of which Ethan had dismissed out of hand because they were too small, and a few ridiculously large beachfront properties Ethan had turned his nose up at because the beach was public property so he'd have no way to stop the general public from accessing it.

Absolute privacy was high on Ethan's list, Niall had discovered. He'd also learned that Ethan's hatred for the color orange bordered on violent, that he considered breakfast the most important meal of the day and therefore required an eat-in kitchen that faced east so he could watch the sunrise, and that he was absolutely helpless without his executive assistant, the self-same woman he'd yelled at earlier about the hotel.

Ethan had called her no less than ten times in the four hours he'd been on the island, forgoing a greeting each time in favor of shooting questions at her rapid-fire. To her credit, Susannah seemed to have a backbone of steel, nonplussed with each call, regardless of whether Ethan was yelling at her about something or engaging her in a heated debate about the merits of a zero-entry pool. Niall assumed it must be standard operating procedure for her; even he, who had only been in Ethan's employ for a few hours, was getting used to his brusque manner and the way his mind seemed to flit from topic to topic with no segue.

They hadn't even stopped long enough to have a real dinner. Ethan, it turned out, wasn't very fond of fancy restaurants, so they'd stopped for curry at a hole-in-the-wall restaurant popular with the locals instead of keeping their reservation at the fancy in-house restaurant at Frenchman's Lookout. Niall felt odd sitting in one of his favorite restaurants wearing wool trousers and an oxford shirt, his suit coat long ago abandoned in concession to the heat. He'd garnered a long, amused look from the owner, who was used to seeing Niall in shorts and ratty T-shirts.

"It doesn't have to be more than one story," Ethan said, motioning widely with a piece of roti he'd dipped in his curry. "It might be nice to have a house wrapped around a courtyard."

Niall forked a bite of rice into his mouth, chewing as he jotted Ethan's preferences down on a piece of paper. There weren't too many more homes he could show him on the island, not in the luxurious range Ethan was looking at.

"How married are you to the idea of living on Tortola itself? There are several smaller islands that might offer more of the privacy you want. Scrub Island is much more exclusive, despite its name."

Ethan snorted into his bottle of Kingfisher. "Scrub Island? Definitely doesn't sound like a place oozing with wealth. Someone dropped the ball in marketing, eh?"

Niall rolled his eyes, surprising himself. He'd never been this relaxed or informal with a client before—especially not one who could bring Niall a commission. Hell, he could afford to buy a bigger boat and go into the charter service again. Keandra would have her real estate license in a few months and he could sell the office to her. With that kind of commission, he'd be able to let her pay him over time and not have it put a strain on either of their finances.

Niall swallowed, the thought of being able to sell the agency making his chest tighten. He'd been an estate agent back home in Kingston upon Hull, but it had never been his life's goal. It had merely been a way to bide his time until Nolan was back from serving in the Royal Marines so the two of them could live out their dream of running a fishing charter in the British Virgin Islands. But Niall had quickly realized after selling his possessions and showing up on Tortola with little more than a suitcase and his captain's license that making a living as a fishing-boat captain was harder than he and Nolan had imagined. Rather than admit defeat and move back home after the first year, Niall had made the decision to leave the boat in the marina and do what he knew he could do well: sell real estate. He'd founded his agency two years ago, hating every moment of it but doing it because he hadn't wanted to admit the plans he and Nolan had made had been fruitless.

"So, Scrub Island?"

Niall looked up at Ethan's prompt, a blush stealing across his tanned cheeks at being caught out daydreaming. Selling the agency, buying a bigger boat—those things wouldn't happen without a fat commission from this sale.

"It's a planned community, basically. It just opened a few months ago, so it's still in the building stages. It's all high-end homes and exclusive resorts, though, so you may find something you'd like. There are a few more homes here on Tortola I'd like to show you tomorrow morning, but if you don't find anything you like, I can run you out to Scrub Island."

"Planned community?" Ethan wrinkled his nose and took another swig of his beer. "No thanks."

"Well, if you object to sharing your beach with tourists, it might be a good way to go."

"I'd try Great Camanoe before that," Ethan said, still looking faintly disgusted.

"Well, I can run you there too."

Ethan squinted in the weak rays of the dying sun, considering Niall's offer.

"You have a boat, then?"

Niall sighed. "I live on a bloody island. Yes, I have a boat."

IT WAS dark by the time Niall pulled up in front of his bungalow, fully expecting some sort of snide commentary from Ethan about its size and general appearance. There was no doubt it was much more rustic than Ethan was accustomed to, but despite that, he didn't say a word. In fact, Ethan didn't say much for the rest of the night, not even when Niall showed him to the small but serviceable guest room and pointed out the bungalow's only bathroom.

It felt strange to Niall to be sleeping in his own bed, as it did every year when he decamped from his monthlong stay on the boat. Even though he'd been the one to purchase it, Niall rarely ever thought of the Orion as his; in Niall's mind, it belonged to both him and Nolan. If Nolan hadn't tried to play the hero in a routine mugging four years ago, the two of them would both be on the Orion's title. Instead, Nolan had died in a dirty alleyway in central London, and Niall had signed the boat paperwork alone. Niall spent the first few months after Nolan's death being angry with him. He'd been absolutely furious with Nolan for intervening when he saw a man holding a knife to a young woman's throat and demanding her purse. But now he'd had the luxury of time to help him start to heal, Niall had come to terms with Nolan's death. He knew there was no way Nolan could have not stepped in and tried to save the girl. As much as losing Nolan hurt, Niall had at least some small comfort knowing Nolan had died doing something that mattered.

Niall usually didn't dwell on the past, but it was four years ago to the day that Nolan had died. Being in the bungalow made it even worse. Though Niall had replaced the entire bedroom suite after he'd moved to the island, the room still felt like it belonged to Nolan. Nolan had picked out the place, finding it on one of the furloughs from the Royal Marines he spent combing the Caribbean for the perfect spot to retire to after he left the military. Niall had come along for the ride each time, but it had been more to see Nolan on his infrequent breaks than it had been to explore the islands looking for a place he and Nolan could start a fishing charter.

They'd had two years together in Hull between Nolan's retirement to the private sector and his death. There had been many loose ends to tie up, and though Nolan owned the house on Tortola, they'd been far from prepared to make the island their permanent home. Niall knew if Nolan had been on his own, he would have left England as soon as the ink had dried on his discharge papers, but Niall had been reluctant to leave the shelter of a well-paid, stable job and the comfort of nearby friends and family.

Niall had wanted to ease into it, save more money for a down payment on a yacht for the charter, build up a nest egg to fall back on if the business didn't pan out. Looking back on it now, he realized Nolan must have been miserable. It made Niall's stomach churn to think about all the opportunities he'd had and wasted. If he'd known Nolan would die, Niall would have moved them to Tortola in a heartbeat. He'd have told his boss to stuff it when he'd asked him to work late. He'd have spent his weekends in bed with Nolan instead of out at open houses and showings. But he hadn't known. He'd thought he and Nolan had a lifetime together, more than enough time to live out Nolan's dream after squaring away all the practicalities first.

But Niall had been the one who'd taken the plunge and bought the boat they couldn't afford. Niall was the one living in Nolan's house, the tiny bungalow Nolan had spent every penny of his share of his gran's inheritance on eight years ago. It had been an extravagance they couldn't afford, and they'd fought bitterly over it when Nolan had purchased it.

Nolan had still been in the service when he'd signed the deed for the house. He'd never gotten the chance to live there, settling for spending a few weeks here and there on Tortola when he could. The house had been his for four years before he died, and the next anniversary of Nolan's death would mark the first year Niall had actually owned it longer than him. Niall wasn't sure how he was going to deal with that. Every year Niall promised himself he'd spend the month somewhere else instead of wallowing on the boat, but he never seemed to be able to actually book a ticket anywhere. Besides, if he couldn't be happy on an island paradise, where could he be happy?

The only vacations Niall had taken in the last few years were to New Jersey to visit Nolan's sister Stephanie and her family. Niall knew she missed Nolan, too, but she'd never shared this part of Nolan's life. Stephanie had been out to Tortola twice, but she wasn't fond of the water and always insisted Niall come to them instead. Niall was sure it was Stephanie's way of making sure he got off the island and away from the shadow of the life he and Nolan should have had, even if only for a few weeks at a time.

Niall didn't mind. For some reason, he took comfort in knowing he had a piece of Nolan no one else did on Tortola.

Stephanie treated Niall like a brother, and he was grateful beyond measure he hadn't lost her along with Nolan. Every time he visited her family in Newark, though, he came away missing Nolan more. It hurt that their niece, Camille—and Niall did think of her as their niece, despite the fact they'd never married, even after having been together for eight years—barely remembered Nolan.

He and Nolan had been younger than Camille was now when they'd met. Nolan had always planned to move to a tropical paradise, even when they'd been small. It wasn't an uncommon dream in the dreary, chilly port town they grew up in, where the water was always too cold to swim and the beaches were made of rocks, not sand. When they'd been twelve, Nolan had started planning out his future, including the luxury yacht he would live on, which they'd decided to name the Millennium Falcon. At seventeen Nolan had decided it would be better to name it Demi Moored, which they'd both thought clever at the time. Nolan and Nolan's dreams of living in the Caribbean had always been a part of his life, and when they'd made the slow, natural transition from friends to lovers, the dream became Niall's, too.

Tongue-in-cheek names for the boat—and later, for the fishing charter company Nolan had decided he'd start—had featured prominently in the weekly e-mails and phone calls Niall and Nolan had shared in the years Nolan had been stationed overseas. None of those names had seemed fitting when Niall finally bought the vessel, using the money from the sale of his townhouse as the down payment on the sleek fifty-foot sportfishing yacht. He'd named it Orion instead, after one of the constellations they both could see while Nolan was in Afghanistan and Niall was in Hull. They'd seen the cartoon An American Tale when they were kids, and the idea that they could look up into the sky and feel close to each other from thousands of miles away had seemed romantic when Nolan had first shipped out. They'd picked the constellation instead of the moon, since Orion was a little harder to spot in the night sky. It meant they had to actually look for it, which had made it more special, they'd reasoned. Niall still caught himself scanning the night sky for it absently, even several years after Nolan's death.

Even water-phobic Stephanie had come out to see Orion launched. They'd broken a bottle of Guinness over its helm instead of the traditional champagne, since the dark ale had been Nolan's favorite brew.

"Vitamin G can cure all that ails you," Nolan had been fond of saying.

It wasn't a coincidence Niall drank a lot of it these days.

THREE

"I'M JUST not sure," Ethan said, narrowing his eyes as he ran a hand along the coarse stucco that covered the exterior walls of the eighth—and last—house Niall had to show him on Tortola.

"It's a single story with a courtyard. Set back from the beach and heavily landscaped for total privacy," Niall said, glancing down at the file folder Keandra had prepared on the colossal eight-acre estate.

"Six bedrooms. Seven bathrooms. A separate guest house with two more bedrooms, two bathrooms and a small kitchen." Niall didn't stop talking as he typed in the security code the selling agent had given him the day before. The door swung open and he stepped inside, not looking back to see if Ethan was following him. After seven other showings, their routine was fairly solid.

"There's a boathouse and a dock, but I don't think either is large enough for your catamaran." That was nothing new. Ethan's seventy-foot catamaran would need to be housed at a marina, especially since it would sit empty most of the year.

"Pool?"

The U-shaped house curved around an enormous tiled courtyard. When the doors were all opened, the courtyard became almost an extension of the house. Niall stepped through one of the arches, leading Ethan to the impressive pool at the courtyard's center.

"Zero entry, obviously," Niall said, consulting his notes. "Apparently the fountain helps circulate the water and make the pool more eco-friendly, since it requires less chemicals."

When Ethan didn't respond, Niall looked up from his file, barely holding back a startled laugh when he saw the fountain, situated at the far end of the rectangular pool where the water was deeper. It was obviously meant to be a sculpture of Venus, but instead of portraying her in the classical marble Roman style, the sculptor had used mosaic tile. The result was vividly colored and borderline pornographic, which was obviously what the artist's intent had been since one of the jets from the fountain hit Venus at a strategic point, if her orgasmic expression was anything to go by.

"Er."

"I don't mind chemicals," Ethan said, his lips twitching.

"I rather think I could use some chlorine now to wipe that image from my brain." Niall laughed, unable to look away from the horrifying sight.

"Let's cross this one off the list."

"You could always have the pool renovated," Niall said, already packing up the file. He'd known Ethan wouldn't be interested in the house the moment they'd stepped inside the front gate. There was something indefinable missing from it, the same thing that had been missing from all the others. He didn't often feel any sort of emotional connection with his clients, but he'd somehow managed to forge one with Ethan. At least, he thought he had. It could also just be good old-fashioned lust.

"I'd still know it had been there," Ethan said with a violent mock shudder. He dipped his sandal-clad toes in the water, looking at the statue with distrust as he tested its temperature. "Water's cold, so they've refilled it recently. Probably means the whole 'less chemicals' thing didn't work out too well."

Niall could see where algae had been scrubbed off the sides of the pool. He had to hand it to Ethan, the man was much more observant than Niall figured the average tech tycoon was. He was also outdoorsy, ruggedly so. Over dinner the night before, they'd talked about Ethan's boat, a catamaran he kept moored in Seattle. Ethan had been living in San Francisco when he'd started his software company, but as soon as he'd made enough money to really get off the ground, he'd moved the entire operation to Seattle. When Ethan described the view of Elliot Bay his house had, Niall had to wonder why he was looking for a vacation home on Tortola. It was obvious Ethan was in love with his home and the city it was in. By the end of their meal, Niall had already accepted Ethan's vague invitation to come visit Seattle some time to go rock climbing, one of Ethan's favorite pastimes. None of the things he'd learned about Ethan so far matched with his mental stereotypes of computer programmers and wealthy CEOs. Ethan was too down-to-earth, too real, to be intimidating anymore, even when he pulled out his phone and barked orders at his minions—Ethan's word for them, not Niall's. He'd choked on his beer the night before when Ethan had casually referenced going hiking in the Hoh Rainforest with his "public relations minion and associate minions." After Niall had confirmed minion wasn't in their actual job title ("Of course not, Niall. They're vice presidents and associate vice presidents, just like at any normal corporate hamster wheel. They only use their minion nameplates at private meetings."), he'd made Ethan tell him about the rainforest, which seemed like such an impossibility tucked into the temperate Pacific Northwest. It was quite a feat for Ethan's description of it to make Niall jealous it wasn't a sight he'd seen, given that Niall lived in an indisputably gorgeous location himself.

All in all, Ethan was not what Niall had been expecting. Niall was finding it increasingly difficult to keep a professional distance. He had a hard and fast rule about hitting on clients. When he'd been younger, still in college and working part time at an estate agent's office in Hull as a filing clerk to help pay his tuition, he'd witnessed what happened when agents slept with their clients. It had been messy and awkward, and he'd learned enough from it to know business and pleasure don't mix, even when business is six foot three and mouthwateringly handsome. Probably especially then, he noted ruefully.

"So, moving on, then?" Niall tucked his file under his arm, giving the statue one final disgusted glance as he rounded the pool and headed back into the cool interior of the house. He'd taken his cues from Ethan this morning, wearing a pair of thin khakis and a golf shirt, but he was still roasting in the humidity. The impending tropical storm had taken care of the baking sun, at least. Niall was grateful for the cloud cover as he led Ethan back to his open-topped Jeep. He borrowed the Mercedes from his neighbor, Mrs. Jim, when he had important clients to ferry around, but when Ethan had seen the Jeep parked under the carport that morning, he'd lobbied to use it instead. Niall had been only too happy to comply; the Jeep navigated the rough, hilly roads that led to the more exclusive neighborhoods much better than Mrs. Jim's aging Mercedes.

Niall briefed Ethan on the homes they'd see on Grand Camanoe as they drove along the winding road that hugged the coast. The water was choppy, but there were still a fair number of boats out enjoying what would probably be the last afternoon of relatively fair weather for a few days, what with Thalia brewing farther out at sea. Ethan commented more than once that the white-capped water and gray skies reminded him of home. Most clients would be upset at being on the island on one of the rare cloudy days Tortola had, but not Ethan.

"Not a bad day to be out there," Ethan said, nodding toward the ocean.

"Could be worse, that's for sure."

"Josh is prone to motion sickness, which one of the reasons I traded in for the catamaran a few years ago." Ethan was oblivious to the way the lines around Niall's mouth hardened a bit. Ethan hadn't mentioned a significant other, but then again, Niall hadn't offered up such personal information about himself, either. He felt like kicking himself for indulging in such flights of fancy. They'd been flirting, but that was probably just Ethan's personality.

Of course Ethan had a boyfriend. Hell, if this Josh had been around "for a few years," it sounded like it was much more serious than merely being a boyfriend. Ethan had a partner, and Niall hadn't even thought to ask. It was usually one of the first things he asked a client, but Ethan had thrown Niall off his usual game.

"Niall?"

Niall turned to look at Ethan, who was squinting at him through a pair of expensive-looking sunglasses. Niall hummed a bit in response, furrowing his brow.

"The trip out to Greater Camanoe? I was asking you how long it takes."

Niall swept his gaze back to the road, hoping the slight glare off the windshield hid his blush. He needed to buckle down and stop daydreaming if he didn't want to lose Ethan as a client. And he definitely didn't. While he was enjoying being out with Ethan, he wasn't particularly enjoying playing the role of interested real estate agent shepherding him through the lavish properties. And if Niall couldn't enjoy that, then he really had no business being a real estate agent at all, did he? The problem was he hadn't particularly enjoyed captaining a fishing charter, either. And he'd obviously been horrible at it, since it hadn't taken more than a year for his savings to run out and necessitate his opening up his own real estate agency to help pay the bills.

"Not long. We can be out there and back by dusk, I'd say. I only have a few properties to show you out on the island."

"Do we have time for a late lunch before heading out? I'm starving." Ethan's stomach gave a weak rumble at the words, and Niall laughed.

"There are a few restaurants here at the marina," he said, easing the Jeep onto the gravel road that led to the parking lot that serviced the small marina. It wasn't anything fancy, but he could afford to keep the Orion moored there, and it had easy access to a few cheap but good restaurants and grocery stores. Certainly there were none of the enormous yachts and catamarans Ethan was used to, but it more than suited Niall's needs. His boat was one of the nicest ones there, and the owners of the marina always took special care to look after it for him while he was away or too busy to come down for regular inspections. Or too wrapped up in self-loathing, which was often the case for most of the month of October, following his self-enforced month-long seaside vigil marking Nolan's death. The owners had never said anything about that, either, and Niall tucked a bit extra into the envelope for his monthly dock fees every Christmas because of their understanding and discretion.

"Why don't I grab a few sandwiches while you gas up, and we can eat them on the way?" Ethan had his feet on the ground before Niall had a chance to take his keys out of the ignition. Niall followed Ethan's gaze toward the small cluster of buildings that ringed the marina. Most of them were little more than shacks, not even equipped with kitchens, the proprietors selling food they'd made at home.

"The marina you'd dock your catamaran at is up the road a bit. It has all the bells and whistles this one's missing. We can stop there on the way back to my place later if you want to see it."

Ethan nodded, pointing at the dockside restaurants with a quizzical tilt of his head. Niall nodded, watching Ethan's confident stride as he made his way over to them like a local.

Niall headed up the dock, grateful for the opportunity to go aboard ahead of Ethan. He knew the galley was a mess since he'd been living in the tiny quarters for two weeks. He dashed around, tidying up the clothes tossed haphazardly over the floor and the old dishes sitting on top of the cherry cabinets. He'd managed to tuck the worst of the mess into the master stateroom when he heard footsteps aboveboard, Ethan's voice carrying on the wind as he called down to tell Niall he'd come aboard.

"Down here, be up in a minute!"

"Everything alright?" Ethan's face appeared at the top of the narrow stairs, his sunglasses tipped up on top of his head.

"Just a bit messy," Niall answered, deciding his hurried efforts had been enough. He climbed the stairs, taking the bag Ethan held out as he ascended.

"Bachelor on a boat, I know how that goes," Ethan said, the corners of his eyes crinkling as he grinned. "All set up here?"

Niall slid behind the helm, making the necessary adjustments on the instrument panel. The boat came to life and Niall turned to Ethan, who'd braced himself near the captain's chair. He'd put his bag of food on the console next to Niall's, and his gaze was trained out to sea like a seasoned boater.

They were both silent as Niall carefully guided the yacht out of its mooring and through the no-wake zone. The short jaunt, as always, felt like it took an interminably long time because of the slow speed. Niall liked to go fast; it was the best thing about captaining a boat, cutting through the waves with the wind roaring around him, feeling the thrill of the vibrations from powerful engines working under the deck. The Albemarle he was driving at the moment, though, was no speedboat. But he'd found even thirty-three knots could be exhilarating out on the open ocean. It felt quite fast for such a large boat, even if it didn't come close to the sensation of actually sitting a bare few inches above the waves, breathing in the spray. Years of learning the art of regatta racing with his father had left Niall with a deep appreciation of both the speed and danger of the sport.

When they'd eased out of the no-wake zone and Niall opened up his speed, Ethan slipped around him to rummage through the bags of food. It was much clearer sailing now; most of the boats had been clustered around the island, keeping close in case the weather turned. Out in the open sea, Niall could only see two other boats, and both were anchored, their owners probably fishing.

He took the thick sandwich Ethan offered him, recognizing the salty bite of cured ham that meant it had to be from Mama Rosio's. Her shop, one of the only ones with a working kitchen in it, looked like a scene out of a Spanish village, with curing hams of different vintages hanging from the ceiling. It was one of Niall's favorite places to go; Mama Rosio was the daughter of Spanish immigrants, and the shop always felt like a slice of Europe. It was hardly a substitute for England, but when he felt homesick, Mama Rosio's was his go-to spot for a taste of, if not home, at least close to home.

"Fridge downstairs?"

Niall nodded, sandwich clenched between his teeth as he used one hand to steer and the other to unfurl a chart on the small console table. Ethan grabbed a third, bigger bag from under the seat.

"Mama Rosio said you needed this," he said, unfurling the crimped top of the brown paper bag.

Before Niall even looked away from his chart, he knew what it was. The unmistakable aroma made his mouth water. Mama Rosio, on occasion, had been known to make him his favorites when she thought he was in a particularly bad funk. Evidently, he'd been frequenting her shop too much in the last few weeks on the boat; she'd made him a shepherd's pie.

"She said it's ground turkey instead of lamb. Apparently, she's worried about your cholesterol." Ethan and Niall both laughed. Niall swallowed his bite, flattening the empty bag over the edge of the chart and laying the sandwich on it to keep it from rolling back up.

"I may have been in there a few too many times lately," Niall said sheepishly, his lips curving into a grin when Ethan laughed again. Niall loved the rich sound of it. Even if Ethan was off the market, so to speak, Niall figured he could still indulge a little in enjoying his company. He hadn't had camaraderie like this with anyone since moving to the island. Jacks was a good companion for a night of drinks and island gossip, and Mrs. Jim doted on him like he was her own, but it wasn't a substitute for actually having friends.

Ethan disappeared downstairs and Niall cringed a little as he remembered shoving an old pizza box and several empty bottles of soda and beer into the refrigerator on his whirlwind attempt at cleaning. He shrugged off the worry, consulting the chart at his side for the coordinates he needed to set his course with the autopilot. He was busy enough for the next five minutes that he didn't realize Ethan hadn't rejoined him after going below to put the shepherd's pie in the refrigerator. Niall squinted at the horizon, making sure there were no obstructions. It wasn't advisable to leave the helm, but he figured out in the open sea with no other boats near it was probably an acceptable risk, especially since his client seemed to have disappeared.

"Ethan?" Niall peered down the steps into the galley, nose wrinkling when he recognized the fake citrus scent of the cleaning spray Niall kept on board.

After giving a final look out toward the horizon to verify it was still clear, Niall clambered down the stairs, mouth open to call for Ethan again. The word died on his lips, and his foot slipped on the last stair, forcing him to grab the railing, when he saw the state of the galley.

Ethan had taken the pizza box and empty cans out of the refrigerator and stacked them neatly in the bin Niall used for recycling. He'd washed the dishes that had been sitting in the sink and left them to dry on a clean towel on the counter, which Ethan had apparently wiped down with the citrus-scented cleaning solution he'd probably found in the cabinet.

Ethan looked up as Niall slipped, eyes full of laughter as he watched Niall scramble for purchase against the slick wall, finally wrapping his fingers around the sturdy cherry railing. Niall took a shuddering breath, his stomach full of butterflies from the almost fall, and then started laughing himself.

"You're cleaning."

Ethan had the grace to look a little chagrined at having been caught out, but Niall couldn't really complain. After all, Ethan was cleaning. It was something Niall did only grudgingly. In fact, he paid a woman to come in and tend to his bungalow once a week, just so he didn't have to scrub floors or wash windows himself. It was a huge indulgence, but without it he'd be living like a pig. The woman always took September off since Niall wasn't around to make a mess, which had led to his panic about the state of the bungalow yesterday. But Ethan obviously didn't share his loathing for chores, since he seemed quite comfortable with the sponge and cleaning bottle in his hands.

"Sorry. I've been told I'm a bit of a neat freak," Ethan said. Niall swallowed hard at the sight of a blush stealing across Ethan's cheeks. He'd only known him for twenty-four hours, but Niall knew he was seeing something rare. Ethan was not the type of man who blushed. Blushing implied discomfort and embarrassment, and if Niall had learned anything about Ethan in their brief acquaintance, it was that Ethan was rarely concerned enough about others' opinions of him to be discomfited.

"By all means, don't let me stop you." Niall winked at Ethan, his heart racing when Ethan's blush deepened. As unwise as it was to be flirting with an unavailable man—who was an important client, to boot—Niall couldn't help himself. It had been a long time since he'd really been able to flirt, and he was enjoying it.

"She's a nice boat." Ethan chucked the sponge into the sink and washed his hands, then dried them on his shirt when he discovered he'd used the only clean towel as a drip catcher for the dishes. "You get her out much?"

"Not as often as I used to," Niall said, rummaging through the refrigerator and coming up with two sodas. He started back up the steps, Ethan at his heels. "When I moved here, I ran a sportfishing charter, but business slowed so much over the winter that I had to give it up."

"How did you get from charter captain to real estate agent?" Ethan popped the top on the soda Niall handed him, leaning a hip lazily against the console while Niall slid back behind the helm, checking his instruments. The autopilot took a lot of the hard work out of navigation, but he still had to be on the lookout, especially with as rough as the sea was turning as Thalia inched closer.

"Actually, I went from estate agent to charter captain," Niall said, keeping his tone light. He didn't like to talk about the reason he'd moved to Tortola and sunk his entire life savings into a boat he couldn't afford so he could take entitled yuppies out to catch fish they had no intention of eating. Maybe he'd use his commission to trade the Orion in for a larger vessel, one more suited to pleasure cruises. He could hire a steward and run private vacation cruises between the islands. There were several boats in that business in the British Virgin Islands, and as far as he could tell, they did well. Of course, everything hinged on getting this commission, which meant Niall needed to stop flirting with Ethan and get his head in the game.

"In Yorkshire?"

Niall startled. Had Ethan run a background check on him? He'd heard of high-level clients being paranoid enough to do that, but Ethan hadn't struck him as that type.

"Your accent. My college roommate was from Bridlington." Ethan's expression was openly curious.

"Hull, just a few miles inland from Bridlington," Niall said, knowing his smile probably looked strained but unable to shake his unease at talking about his past.

"Would that be Kingston upon Hull?" Niall saw concern flit across Ethan's face when Niall flinched, but Ethan continued on. "I've never understood the naming conventions in the UK. Why name it something so burdensome if you're just going to call it Hull? Why not just call it Hull and be done with it?"

Niall took the lifeline, recognizing it for what it was. Apparently, Ethan was compassionate as well as witty, intelligent, and attractive as hell. Not to mention that he liked to clean. Niall suppressed an inward groan as he let himself be drawn into a heated discussion about the British and their sense of formality and propriety. When Ethan threw his head back and laughed at something Niall said, the tanned column of his throat exposed to the sliver of sunlight that had broken through the clouds and refracted off the water, Niall knew he was screwed.

FOUR

As Niall had expected, Ethan hadn't liked any of the homes he'd shown him on Grand Camanoe. Ethan had only allotted two days to be in Tortola, which meant he'd be heading back to Seattle the next morning empty-handed. Niall had at least gotten Ethan to complete the mandatory paperwork the British Virgin Islands required in order to purchase property; it would take about six months to get the final permit, but at the rate they were going, Ethan probably wouldn't even have found a home by then.

"We should head back to Tortola," Niall told Ethan as he eased the loaner car into the last spot in the Grand Camanoe public marina parking lot. Thalia was building, and many boat owners were there to secure their boats to ride out the storm. Those with smaller vessels would load them up and bring them ashore for safekeeping, while those with boats the size of Niall's would be sailing them into a sheltered cove while they waited for the storm to pass over. Niall had been checking the weather as he'd ferried Ethan from one home to the next, and there was no doubt Thalia was about to come ashore.

The rain started just as Niall turned the headlights off. Through Jacks, he'd managed to rent a car from an islander for the day; Niall hoped the man was able to come pick it up before Thalia really kicked up. The marina parking lot on Grand Camanoe regularly flooded when there was a severe tropical storm, and it looked like Thalia might make it up to a low-grade hurricane. He winced at the thought of his own Jeep back in the lot at Tortola. At least he'd had the presence of mind to zip the top up. Not that it would matter if the engine got flooded.

Niall grimaced when he remembered he hadn't thought to bring any rain ponchos with him. Umbrellas were useless in the wind, not that he had one of those, either. With a grim nod at Ethan, Niall grabbed his satchel full of files and opened the door, surprised at the strength of the wind as it pushed the heavy metal back at him.

"Sorry! Thalia must be blowing in faster than the meteorologists expected," he yelled at Ethan as the two of them started to sprint toward the dock, hunched over to protect their faces from the driving rain.

"Feels just like home!" Ethan yelled back, letting out a loud whoop as he lifted his face to the rain. "Except warmer!"

They managed the ladder without much trouble, but the deck was slick enough for them to slide as they hurried across it. The rain was loud against the roof of the shelter that enclosed the helm, its drumming audible even over the roaring wind.

Even with his hair plastered to his head and his light-blue shirt soaked to the point of transparency, Ethan looked like some sort of model in an outdoor living advertisement. His eyes were dancing with amusement, his smile natural and warm. Looking at him, it was easy for Niall to forget the discomfort of his wet, squishy shoes and the rivulets of water running from his sodden clothes.

It was not, however, so easy to dismiss the warning from the National Oceanic and Atmospheric Administration's hurricane center, which was advising all vessels in the British Virgin Islands to seek shelter from the storm. Niall scrolled through the message on his phone, reaching out to tune the ship's radio to the alert station. Sure enough, the automated voice was advising against open sea travel for boats of Orion's size.

"Shit."

Niall looked over at Ethan, surprised to find him on the phone. Until that moment he hadn't realized Ethan hadn't taken a single call all afternoon, not since they'd set out for Grand Camanoe. He'd heard Ethan's phone buzz several times, but the other man hadn't taken any of the calls, simply scowling at what Niall assumed were text messages in response to the missed calls. He didn't know what to make of it; Ethan had been glued to that phone since his arrival. Niall had been so caught up in the easy conversation and flirting, it had seemed natural for Ethan's attentions to be fixed solely on him, but now that Niall had a moment to really think about it, it seemed strange.

"You're sure?" Ethan waved toward Niall, miming writing on something. Niall scrounged around in the small drawer of the console, coming up with a napkin and a pen. Ethan took them, his wet hand smudging the ink as he scrawled something on the napkin. "Thanks. Yeah, we will. You too."

"Thalia's about to be upgraded to a Cat 2 hurricane," Ethan said, thrusting the soggy napkin across the small table so Niall could read it. "This is apparently the best cove to take shelter in here on Grand Camanoe."

"We don't have time to make it back to Tortola?" Niall already knew the answer, of course, but he was curious who Ethan had been on the phone with. The radio hadn't said anything about reclassifying Thalia.

"Nope. It may be dicey even getting to that cove." Ethan looked out over the growing swells, a line forming between his brows as he frowned.

Niall glanced down at the name of the cove. "I was planning to head out to—"

"The other coves and harbors are on the wrong side of Thalia," Ethan said, scanning the chart Niall had left out to find the cove in question. "This one has a hurricane hole. And Thalia will be upgraded to a hurricane."

Ethan looked up, squinting as he examined the pylons the yacht was currently moored to. "Or we could stay here. Is this marina hurricane safe?"

Staying in the marina had the added benefit of allowing the two of them to weather the storm on land, but from the way the other owners were hurriedly loading up their boats and the empty larger berths, Niall didn't figure the Orion had a good chance of coming through Thalia unscathed if he left her moored there. Of course, that didn't mean he had to condemn Ethan to a potentially disastrous night on a rough sea. A Category 2 hurricane wasn't enough to do widespread damage, but it was enough to wreck a boat.

"No. And besides, I don't have any of my supplies." Stupid, Niall thought, to not bring his hurricane kit when setting out ahead of a tropical storm. He'd be paying for it now.

At least Ethan had a way to get inland. Niall had left the keys to the car he'd borrowed for the day in the glove box, which would be dangerous most other places, but crime in the islands was almost nonexistent, especially among the locals. Everyone who saw the car would know it was Old Charlie's, and it wasn't as though someone could steal it and not be noticed.

"Alright, I'll take Orion out to that cove," Niall agreed, which was unnecessary because Ethan was already loading the coordinates into his autopilot's GPS. "If you've got everything handled up here, I'll go below and get you some dry clothes to take with you. I'm sure I have something that'll do."

"May as well wait until we've reached the cove and dropped anchor before changing." Ethan squinted at the control panel, evidently struggling with the unfamiliar console. "We'll just get soaked again doing it."

Niall frowned. "You're not coming with me. You're driving inland and finding a hotel."

Ethan arched an eyebrow at him, and Niall felt his belly heat at the supercilious look. He wondered if there was ever a time Ethan took orders. He'd very much like to find out. A big swell knocked the boat against the pylons it was tethered to, making Niall remember the precarious situation they were in. He felt like a teenage boy, his arousal on a hair trigger. He should be getting ready to navigate the boat out to the hurricane hole—without Ethan on it—not wondering if Ethan would beg or whimper underneath him. It was probably the adrenaline, Niall reasoned.

"Ethan, I don't know if you've ever been on a boat in rough weather like this—"

"We do have hurricanes in the Pacific, you know."

"Not like we do here," Niall said, pinching the bridge of his nose. Suddenly he was aware of how tired he was. Tired, wet, cold, hungry, and in no position to argue with someone who wanted to help.

"Fine." Before he could get a look at Ethan's no-doubt triumphant expression, Niall headed out to untie the boat. He didn't have time to waste arguing with Ethan, especially knowing the special brand of stubbornness Ethan seemed to call his own. If Ethan wanted to spend his night getting tossed around a boat, who was Niall to argue? He worked the rope with more force than necessary, his lips twisted into a grim line. Niall was fairly sure that by morning, Ethan would be seasick and sorry he hadn't stayed on land. Assuming they didn't capsize and drown, of course.

The thought of being responsible for Ethan getting hurt was sobering, and Niall finished getting the boat ready to set sail, preparing his renewed argument to get Ethan somewhere safe. This wasn't like rock climbing or sky diving or any of the other thrill-seeker pursuits he knew Ethan liked; the risk of getting hurt was very real. He would convince Ethan to seek shelter on shore, no matter what the cost to his own pride. If he had to beg him, he would. Of course, the easiest way to convince Ethan to get off the boat would be to get off the boat himself, but Niall wasn't prepared to go quite that far. The Orion would get battered to pieces if she was moored when Thalia's storm surge came in.

31

"Listen, Ethan—" Niall's protest died on his lips as he rounded the corner and saw Ethan, shirtless and in his bare feet, securing everything he could on the deck with the thick white nylon rope Niall kept on board for exactly that purpose. Things that could easily blow away had already been piled into the berth downstairs and Niall could see a roll of duct tape circling Ethan's wrist. He was obviously planning to tape all the windows next.

Rain beaded against Ethan's chest, which was as tanned and toned as his arms and legs. Niall had gotten a glimpse of Ethan's tantalizing forearms at the airport the day before, but that hadn't prepared him for the utter perfection of Ethan's chest and stomach. It was obvious he worked out, and outside, at that. Could you rock climb shirtless, Niall wondered, his mouth going dry when Ethan reached up and braced himself on the bit of roof that hung over the helm, his back muscles flexing as he effortlessly pulled himself up, his bare feet planted on the console. Niall watched, transfixed, as Ethan ripped a piece of tape off the roll with his teeth, one hand still hanging on to the roof as he stuck the tape to the glass, using it to reinforce the seams of the window.

Two things were clear to Niall in that moment: one, Ethan was no stranger to bad weather at sea and would likely be an asset to have on board rather than a liability, and two, the hurricane brewing just off the stern was the least of Niall's problems at the moment.

Taping finished, Ethan dismounted from the console table, feet steady and sure even as the wet deck pitched underneath him in the waves. He turned and saw Niall, teeth flashing as he shot him an exhilarated grin. It was obvious Ethan was enjoying himself.

"All set?" The wind was strong enough now that though they were only a few feet apart, Ethan's words were lost. Niall had been watching his mouth, though, tracking the movement of his full lower lip, so he knew what he'd said. He nodded, woodenly moving forward toward the helm. There was no relief as the roof shielded him from the driving rain, though, because Ethan crowded in next to him, body wet and radiating heat.

"The shirt was just getting in my way," Ethan explained, leaning back and shaking the water out of his short hair. Niall looked down at his own shirt, which seemed to have gained about five pounds in the torrential downpour. Even though he was uncomfortable, he didn't follow suit and take it off. It was hard enough to concentrate with Ethan standing half-naked next to him; he didn't need to be able to feel the warmth of Ethan's sun-browned skin inches from his own naked chest.

"And the shoes?"

"All the rock climbing. I have toes of steel. It was easier to grip the deck without the shoes."

Niall shook his head, turning on the boat's windshield wipers so he could see. It didn't help much; the rain was coming down in sheets now, making it impossible to see more than a few feet off the stern. He turned the engines over, feeling apprehension instead of the usual exhilaration at the rumble of the powerful machine under his feet.

"Here goes nothing," he said, guiding the boat out of its moorings and toward the cove Ethan had suggested.

Niall's knuckles were white by the time they made it to the hurricane hole. His fingers ached from where they'd been clenched around the steering wheel. Ethan's excitement appeared to wane a bit as they navigated the growing swells, but he was still obviously enjoying himself. They hadn't spoken since the Orion had left the marina because Niall needed to concentrate fiercely on keeping them on course and watching for other boats doing the same thing. There were about five other yachts weathering the storm around them, at anchor in the hurricane hole Ethan had found, which Niall figured meant it was probably a good choice.

Niall piloted them into the deepwater cove, bringing the boat as close to the shoreline as he dared. He was careful not to come close to another boat, knowing Thalia would likely toss the Orion around in the night. Through the driving rain, he could just make out the shoreline ringed around them. There were no houses visible:

only a thick forest of tall trees that would help block the wind. The sea was too rough to try tying the boat off now, but later when they were in the hurricane's eye, he could swim ashore and tie the boat to the trees if the anchors weren't holding it well.

"Drop anchor?" Ethan yelled, already outside the meager shelter of the roof.

"Both in the bow," Niall answered, nodding toward the starboard side of the hull. Ethan set off for it immediately, while Niall fought his way against the wind toward the port side of the bow. His fingers slipped over the wet rope as he worked, his brow furrowed in concentration. Even with his feet firmly planted about a shoulder's width apart, Niall was getting battered by the fierce wind. He finally worked the anchor free, tossing it over the side as far away from the boat as he could. It disappeared under the roiling water, the spool whirling quickly as it fed the anchor rope. Niall didn't realize he'd been holding his breath until the spool stopped. He just hoped the anchor had taken hold on the bottom and not a shelf.

FIVE

THE WALK back to the helm was easier with the wind at his back. Niall wiped the rain off his face, eyes stinging from the salty spray. Ethan joined him a minute later, giving him a thumbs-up. Taking a deep breath, Niall turned the engines on, reversing a bit until he felt the anchor lines go taut. The engine growled as the boat came to a standstill, and only then did Niall let himself smile. He turned the engines off, satisfied both anchors had taken firmly, and started to dismantle the console. He began removing all the electronics, as well as anything that might get damaged by water if swells overtook the bow.

Once they were safely belowdecks, both men started the arduous process of securing things in the galley and cabin. The Orion would likely get tossed roughly when Thalia passed over, which meant anything breakable had to be secured so it couldn't move. The furniture was already bolted to the floor, so it wasn't a concern, but Niall had dishes in the cabinets and small appliances that would be ruined if they weren't safeguarded.

Niall was surprised at how competent Ethan was at stowing things away on an unfamiliar boat. The principle was the same on all large craft, but the hidey-holes for things varied by manufacturer. Ethan had no compunction about opening and closing cabinets and drawers until he found what he needed, and Niall appreciated that.

From the look of things on the radar, Thalia was going to be on top of them at any minute.

"Tape?"

Ethan took the roll off his wrist, winging it across the galley at Niall, who caught it easily and immediately started taping things down that couldn't be stowed elsewhere before shoring up the windows in the same way Ethan had done upstairs at the helm.

Niall thought it felt almost anticlimactic when they'd finished and were standing in the middle of the salon, panting with exertion, and nothing happened. The boat was pitching to and fro, and he could still hear the wind howling outside, to say nothing of the driving rain, but it seemed their hurried efforts at finding a safe place to drop anchor and weatherproofing the boat had been successful.

"Christ on a crutch, I need a beer," Ethan said, leaning against the galley's cabinets.

"No shit." Niall paused, hand on the refrigerator. "Dry clothes first?"

Ethan laughed, looking down at his once well-pressed Dockers, which were now so wet they hung off his hipbones, the weight of the sodden fabric pulling them down. Niall followed his gaze automatically, throat going tight as he saw how dangerously low the pants were dipping. He could see the sharp points of Ethan's hips and the barest hint of the ridge of hard muscle disappearing into the waistband. A sprinkling of soft dark hair started at his bellybutton, thickening along the flat planes of his abdomen and giving Niall a good idea of what he'd find if he stepped forward and unbuttoned the khakis.

Niall felt the warm arousal he'd managed to dismiss earlier building again, and he had to force himself to tear his gaze away from Ethan's ruined trousers. The boat lurched underneath them, sending Ethan tumbling into Niall, pinning him to the refrigerator.

"Definitely dry clothes first," Niall said, hoping Ethan hadn't heard the small hitch in his voice. Ethan was overwhelmingly close and unmistakably male. His skin smelled like wood smoke and sunshine on top of the sweet, fresh smell of the rain, and Niall felt his body responding instantly.

"How about no clothes first?" The predatory words were matched by the greedy gleam in Ethan's eyes, the last thing Niall saw before the full lips he'd been admiring all day descended on his own.

Ethan kissed like he did everything else, skillfully and with brute force. His hot tongue licked along the seam of Niall's mouth, demanding entrance, and Niall parted his lips before he had a chance to think about it. Niall heard a hoarse groan when Ethan's tongue delved into his mouth, and seconds later was mortified to realize he had been the one making the desperate and wanton noise. His embarrassment was enough to have him pulling away, giving his mind a chance to catch up with his body, which was raring to go.

"But, no. Stop." Niall stammered and ducked his head as Ethan lowered his lips again, moving out of range. "We shouldn't. Ethan, we can't."

Ethan chuckled. With their chests pressed together, Niall could feel the laugh rumble through his own body. His cock gave a sharp throb as though asking why he was protesting when what he'd been thinking about all day was right there, pressed up against him, all hard muscle and soft angles and warm, wet skin. He felt Ethan's hot breath ghost along his neck, his only warning before Ethan's lips curved against him, mouth sucking at the tender skin of Niall's neck.

"Ethan, I—" Niall lost his already precarious balance when the boat shifted violently in the swells outside, sending both of them tumbling to the floor. It was enough to break Ethan's concentration, and Niall saw the moment rational thought flickered back into Ethan's gorgeous eyes.

"You aren't dating anyone, are you?" The words were sharp, accusatory.

"Me?" Niall recoiled, the cool metal of the refrigerator biting through his wet shirt, making him shiver despite himself.

"I don't have any patience for cheaters," Ethan said coolly. A hot burst of jealously tore through Niall, making him wonder who had hurt Ethan badly enough to make him sound like that.

"Me?" Niall repeated, his voice louder this time. "How about you? What about Josh?" The words were embarrassingly breathless, but Niall didn't care. He'd been a lot of things in his life, but "the other man" was not among them. He didn't sleep with men who were attached to someone else. No matter how much he wanted to, and especially not with someone who was so hypocritical, sitting there lecturing Niall about fidelity when he was about to cheat on his own partner.

"Josh doesn't care who I date. As long as it doesn't interfere with our weekends, why would he?"

"I don't care if you have an open relationship or not, I don't—"

"An open relationship?" Ethan's voice rose an octave, cutting through the haze of arousal that had made it so difficult for Niall to remember why he wasn't supposed to be throwing himself at the hard body in front of him.

"I don't have any sort of relationship with Josh. Jesus, Niall, he's seventeen! I've known him since he was eight!"

Niall gaped at him, stunned. Josh was seventeen? But, no, Ethan had said—

"I'm his mentor," Ethan continued, oblivious to Niall's dawning horror at how badly he'd misjudged the situation. "A volunteer assigned to offer him guidance and companionship? You know, positive male role model?"

When Niall continued to gape, Ethan rolled his eyes. "Do they not have programs like that in England? Disadvantaged city kids, usually fatherless, paired with someone they can look up to?"

"I know what a mentoring program is, Ethan," Niall snapped, cheeks heating.

"Then you also know that Josh is like a son to me. Not a lover." Niall nodded, fighting the urge to flee. Only the knowledge that there wasn't anywhere to go stopped him. The Orion was a good-sized yacht, but she was still tiny belowdecks. Aside from the salon, where they were, there was a small master suite and an even-smaller guest quarters, both of them visible from where they were sitting. There was nowhere for Niall to hide unless he braved Thalia and went on deck. The boat gave an ominous lurch as he was considering it.

"Niall, God." Ethan laughed, apparently giving himself over to the ridiculousness of the situation.

Niall managed a small, embarrassed smile, leaning harder against the refrigerator and wishing it could swallow him whole. Now that his arousal had been completely curbed, he felt cold, wet, and ridiculous. He wanted to go change into dry clothes, get something warm to eat, and definitely have that beer. And then forget this had ever happened.

Not that it sounded like Ethan, who currently had his head thrown back laughing, was likely to let that happen.

"Josh. That's—you've thought that all along? Why were you flirting so shamelessly with me, then?"

Niall blushed darker. "It's alright to flirt. Even if you were taken, it's alright to look. For me. Because I'm single." Niall managed a weak glare, his lips already starting to curve up into a reluctant smile. It was impossible not to laugh along with Ethan; his laugh was beautiful, just like the rest of him.

"But you thought I was some lecher for flirting back, eh?" Ethan responded, answering the unspoken accusation in Niall's words. He laughed again, hoisting himself gracefully up from his kneeling position. He offered Niall a hand and Niall took it reluctantly, stomach jumping at the way Ethan's warm palm felt under his own.

As soon as Niall had regained his footing, Ethan tugged on their joined hands, pulling Niall until he was flush with Ethan's body from chest to thigh.

"I don't cheat." He captured Niall's lips, catching him unawares. Before he could delve his tongue between Niall's lips again, Niall pulled back, face serious as he studied Ethan.

"I don't either. And I've never really done this." He used the hand that wasn't still captured in Ethan's to motion between the two of them.

"Flirt?" Ethan's voice was soft, but Niall knew there was more to the question.

"Have casual sex."

Ethan's grin turned predatory, and Niall's stomach dropped more than could be attributed to the boat being tossed around by the growing waves.

"That sounds like a challenge."

Niall couldn't help but smile. He should have known Ethan would react to his statement that way. But he'd said it because it was true. He wasn't a one-night stand kind of guy.

Niall opened his mouth to respond, but whatever he was about to say was lost when the boat pitched violently, sending both him and Ethan sprawling. The motion of the boat righting itself was nearly as bad. By the time everything had settled, Niall's head was bleeding from where he'd hit the corner of the cabinets, and Ethan had the beginnings of a marvelous black eye from slamming into Niall's knee.

"Shit. This is—shit. We should have gone ashore," Niall muttered, touching his head and blinking in surprise when his fingers came away wet with blood.

"Niall, fuck. Are you alright?" Ethan wobbled up onto his knees, crawling toward Niall. The tape they'd put on the cupboard doors had held, so the floor was clear of debris. Something to be grateful for, Niall thought. He'd heard the tinkling of glass as the dishes broke inside the cabinets when the boat had been thrown.

"Niall? Can you hear me?"

Niall blinked, surprised at how close Ethan's face suddenly was. He felt woozy, like someone had taken out half his brain and replaced the gap with cotton. Or maybe steel wool, he amended as his skull began to throb.

"Yeah, yes." He batted away Ethan's hands in annoyance as the other man tried to run them over him, looking for broken bones. "Stop. I'm fine."

Ethan sat back on his heels, one eye already swelling shut as the other squinted at Niall critically.

"You need some ice for that," Niall said, grimacing as he struggled to get up. The pounding in his head increased tenfold when he stood, making his vision gray out around the edges and leaving him gasping, hands gripping the same counter he'd bashed his head on. One hand slipped a bit, and he looked down, aghast to see there was blood on the countertop, too.

"Forget me. You're bleeding, Niall. We need to get you to a hospital. You could have a concussion."

Niall privately thought there was a good chance he did, but he didn't say it out loud. It wouldn't matter anyway; with Thalia in full gale, there was no way they were going anywhere.

"There's a first aid kit under the bench," Niall said, motioning toward the seats under the window. "Get me some gauze. And maybe some aspirin."

He staggered to the refrigerator while Ethan dug through the provisions in the bench. There wasn't much in the small freezer, but he managed to grab a few handfuls of ice. The dilemma of not having clean kitchen towels was solved when Niall remembered there were towels in the head, so he braced one arm against the wall, using it to steady himself as the boat pitched and curved underneath him. He didn't realize Ethan had followed him in until he felt tentative fingers at his hairline, tracing the blood up until they found the sizable lump above his temple.

Niall hissed in a breath when Ethan's fingers skated gingerly over the lump, mapping its contours. The gash itself wasn't overly large, though it bled copiously. Niall split the ice in his hand between two clean washcloths, intending to hand one to Ethan for his eye, but Ethan stopped him, dumping both in the small sink.

"We need to get your cut washed out first," he said, biting his lower lip as he fished through the first aid kit he'd brought into the bathroom with him. He pulled out some antibiotic ointment as well as the gauze Niall had asked for, but when he reached for the alcohol wipes, Niall shook his head. He groaned, the motion making his head spin even more.

"Soap and water first, then this," Ethan said. When Niall tried to shake his head again, Ethan pushed him down until he was sitting on the lid of the toilet. "Don't be a baby."

Niall rested his head obediently on the cool edge of the sink as Ethan competently washed the blood off his face and out of his hair, holding the wet washcloth to the gash with one hand as he found the alcohol wipe with the other and ripped it open with his teeth.

Instead of swiping the wipe over his cut, Ethan surprised Niall by crouching down in front of him, releasing the washcloth and bringing both hands down to cup his jaw. He traced the slight stubble with his thumbs, holding Niall's gaze as though he was measuring his pupils. Niall tensed when Ethan shifted, then immediately relaxed when Ethan closed the small distance between them and brushed his lips gently against Niall's in an almost chaste kiss. When Niall deepened the kiss, Ethan brought the hand holding the alcohol wipe up, dabbing it against the cut on Niall's temple tenderly.

Niall hissed but didn't break the kiss, his sharp teeth nipping a bit at Ethan's full lower lip in retaliation. After a few more moments, Ethan pulled away with obvious reluctance, grinning when Niall glared weakly at him.

"Not fair."

"I never said I played fair," Ethan said, shaking his head. He winced at the motion, and Niall's head throbbed in sympathy.

They stayed silent as Ethan spread the antibiotic ointment over the cut with soft touches, obviously trying his hardest not to hurt Niall. The gash really did look better once the blood had been washed away, and Niall could tell the moment Ethan realized it wasn't as bad as they'd thought and relaxed a bit. Once he'd applied the gauze and taped it in place, ignoring Niall's protests that taking the bandage off the next day was going to hurt more than the actual injury had, Ethan retied the make-shift ice packs Niall had made and placed one over his own eye, handing the other to Niall to hold on his head.

Niall wished he had a weather report in front of him. The boat had been pitching around for what felt like ages, and he was curious to see if Thalia was directly overhead yet or if things might actually get worse. He wasn't sure what the plan was if the boat capsized, but he was starting to think they should probably have one.

"Bed might be the safest place," Ethan offered, snorting when Niall's eyes widened. "I was just referring to the lack of sharp edges and the ability to be prone."

Niall knew Ethan's put-upon tone was an act designed to make him smile. The obvious ploy made something inside his chest squirm a bit. Niall had only felt this kind of ease with one other person in his life, and the comparison made him uncomfortable.

"Come on, Casanova." Ethan wrapped an arm around Niall's waist and helped him stagger to a standing position. The boat's motions were still jerky, and Niall wondered at that rate how long the anchors would hold. There was still quite a bit of slack, which accounted for the boat's thrashing, and Niall could only hope it was enough to counter the inevitable storm surge.

Niall let Ethan help him into the master suite, grimacing when he saw the mess of clothes on the unmade bed. For a self-proclaimed neat freak, the way Ethan managed to push it all aside without a second glance to deposit him on the bed was impressive, Niall thought.

Niall was already more than halfway asleep by the time Ethan came back with two life jackets, which Niall knew was a worrying development. Niall had taken enough basic first aid classes to know people with serious head injuries should stay awake for several hours. Plus he doubted sleeping while on a boat in the middle of a hurricane was a good idea even if he was in perfect health.

He let Ethan drag him into a sitting position, obediently looping his arms through the life vest when Ethan held it open. If they did need to try to swim for shore, they wouldn't have a prayer of making it without the help of a flotation device. Even then, with the rough water and the huge swells, Niall didn't really like their chances. The Orion was holding strong so far, though, and Niall was hopeful they wouldn't have to worry about it. Once Ethan had both of them buckled into the bright-orange vests, he shook Niall gently, trying to wake him all the way up.

"Come on. Honestly, Niall, I hate it when I have to do all the work in bed."

"Wha—?"

Ethan's laugh sounded like pure relief. Niall forced his eyes to blink open, immediately shutting them again when his headache pulsed.

"Lights."

Ethan let Niall slump back against the headboard as he stretched to flick the switch and plunge the small room into darkness. There was a small window on the other side of the room, near the built-in bureau, bathing the room in an eerie gloom.

"Lights are out. Open your eyes, Niall."

Niall opened them reluctantly, pain stabbing his eyes even from the faint light from outside. He watched Ethan fighting with his cell phone, obviously trying to make a call.

"Too far out of range, even without the storm," Niall muttered, scooting up so his shoulders rested against the headboard as well. It helped the ache in his head a bit. "Not a lot on this side of the island. No towers."

Ethan made a wordless sound of disgust, and Niall laughed. The chuckle set a fresh wave of throbbing off behind his temples, but he didn't wince; he was getting used to it. And really, he'd had worse. This was a walk in the park compared to the time he'd been struck in the head by a wayward mast on his father's sailboat and thrown overboard.

Niall started to sit up, his breath huffing out when Ethan laid a strong hand on his chest, holding him down.

"Radio's in the other room," Niall protested.

"Then I'll go get it." Ethan pursed his lips. There was enough light in the room for Niall to see Ethan narrow his eyes as he stared at him.

"I'll stay here. Fine," Niall said, lowering his voice to mutter, "I'm not some kind of goddamn damsel in distress," as Ethan stalked out of the room.

"As long as that makes me the knight in shining armor!" Ethan called back from the galley.

"It makes you something, that's for sure," Niall yelled back, cringing at the way his headache surged when he raised his voice.

Relaxing back against the headboard, Niall realized the boat didn't seem to be pitching around quite as much as it had been. He wondered if it was because he wasn't as dizzy as he'd been before or because the storm had lessened.

With one eye on the door, Niall leaned over and shook a few more aspirin tablets out of the first aid kit Ethan had brought into the room, swallowing them down before Ethan returned with the radio. Niall didn't want Ethan to know his head hadn't really gotten much better. He checked his watch. It had been almost an hour since he'd fallen. Given that his vision wasn't blurry anymore and he had no other symptoms than a raging headache, he was pretty sure he didn't have a concussion. He felt a bone-weary tiredness that could be chalked up either to the head injury or the fact it was after one in the morning. He hoped it was the latter.

"Eye's passing," Ethan said, fiddling with the knobs on the small radio. As he came closer, Niall could hear the automated voice droning on about wind speeds and admonishments to take cover.

"We could try to sail back to the marina and get to land," Niall offered, half hoping Ethan took him up on it. The Orion would likely be damaged if it was tethered to a pylon, but at least the incessant swaying would stop.

"Doubt we have enough time for that."

Niall blinked, watching Ethan unbuckle his pants. The realization that he was still in his wet clothes, though they were only stiff and damp by now, hit him moments before he started to shiver.

"For Christ's sake, Niall," Ethan growled, advancing on the bed in just his boxers, apparently having heard the brief moment Niall's teeth chattered before he'd clamped down his jaw tightly enough to stop them.

"Get out of those clothes and under the covers. I'm going to swim ashore and set the other two anchors."

"The hell you are." Headache be damned, Niall sat up, swinging his legs over the side of the bed. "The Orion's anchors have held just fine, Ethan. We don't need to tie off."

Ethan shrugged, moving forward and tugging at the ties on Niall's life jacket. He'd already shucked his own off. When Niall didn't protest, Ethan slid the life jacket off his shoulders and then moved to the hem of Niall's shirt. Niall raised his arms automatically, letting Ethan ease the damp fabric over his head, careful not to jostle the bandage. When the cool air hit his damp skin, Niall shivered again, a line of goose flesh erupting over his chest.

Ethan hooked an arm around Niall's torso, pulling him up to stand. He deftly unfastened Niall's trousers one-handed, and Niall took a second to be impressed at Ethan's skill at undressing another person before reason crashed back and he remembered Ethan wasn't undressing him in a fit of passion, he was getting the wet clothes off of him so he could tuck Niall into bed while swimming to shore by himself to secure the boat.

Shudders wracked Niall's body again when Ethan eased the wet trousers down his thighs and let them puddle on the floor. Niall's boxers were damp, too, but Ethan seemed resolute in ignoring them, applying pressure against Niall's chest so Niall had to sit back on the mattress.

"Don't go."

Ethan gave Niall a hooded look, and Niall knew in that moment he couldn't bear it if Ethan jumped over the side of the boat. Though the water was relatively calm in the eye, conditions could change at any second. The rough swells had decreased in frequency, but they were still there, rocking the boat at random intervals. In calm water, he was sure Ethan could easily make the swim. But right now, exhausted and cold, with a rough ocean against him, Niall didn't think Ethan stood a chance. Of course, there was no way he could say that. It would be tantamount to challenging Ethan to defend his manhood and do it. Men like Ethan weren't thrill-seekers because they enjoyed the adrenaline; they were thrill-seekers because they needed the adrenaline. Niall knew the type well; Nolan had been the same way.

Niall gave up fighting his shivers, letting them wrack his body. He really was cold, but he was certain crawling under the blankets would warm him up enough. He didn't want Ethan to know that, though. As he'd hoped, Ethan cradled Niall closer, sharing his body heat with him. Fresh goose flesh sprang up on the side of Niall's body that wasn't pressed against Ethan's warm, tanned skin. Ethan muttered a curse under his breath and reached behind them to grab the edge of the comforter.

"Get under."

Niall complied with Ethan's brusque order, scooting over until there was room enough for Ethan as well. It clearly hadn't been

Ethan's plan to join him, but the boat kicked up in another large swell at that moment, solidifying Niall's resolve. He gave a huge shiver, fake this time, and curled in on himself, trying to look as pathetic as possible. It hurt his pride to play the part of the damsel, but if it kept Ethan safe, he would do it.

Ethan's eyes clouded with real worry, and Niall felt a twinge of guilt about overplaying his condition. When Ethan seemed to come to some sort of internal resolve and climbed in beside him, Niall had to hide his smile by burrowing into the thin, summer-weight duvet.

"Scoot back."

Niall obeyed, spooning up to Ethan's warmth. He really had been cold, and the furnace-like heat Ethan exuded felt like heaven. He couldn't help but let out a contented groan, snuggling back as far as he dared.

Ethan brought an arm around Niall's waist, the flat of his palm grazing the skin above his boxers. Despite his headache, Niall felt his body hum in response. He flexed contentedly when he felt the light press of Ethan's lips against his naked shoulder.

"The life jackets—"

"The radio says the eye will be over us for another forty minutes or so. Let's get you warmed up, and then we can put them back on when the wall starts to pass. It's not like it won't be obvious."

Niall blinked sleepily, knowing he should stay awake but unable to care, bracketed in the comfortable warmth of Ethan's arms with the soft mattress underneath them.

"I'll wake you before things get rough again," Ethan whispered against his ear, his breath stirring the short hairs on the back of Niall's neck.

"Shouldn't."

"I think you're alright, and it's only for a few minutes."

THE NEXT time Niall woke, someone was pressing sucking kisses behind his ear. He groaned and pushed back against the warm body behind him, disoriented enough to think it was Nolan. This was one of Niall's favorite ways to wake up, and he let himself sink into the comfort of it and the slow curl of arousal unfurling in his stomach before realizing it couldn't be Nolan. He jolted, eyes flying open as his mind reeled and tried to process what was happening. He was on the boat. The hurricane. With Ethan.

Niall swallowed back a wave of guilt at his disloyalty, though he couldn't explain who he'd felt disloyal to. To Ethan, for immediately thinking he was Nolan? Or to Nolan, for finding pleasure with Ethan? Niall's head throbbed, and he forced the thoughts aside, focusing on Ethan's lips, which had disappeared from his neck the moment he'd tensed up. It looked to be a little lighter in the room. Niall blinked blearily, realizing Ethan had turned on the bedside reading lamp.

"Eye's just about passed," Ethan said, easing Niall into a sitting position and handing him a life jacket. "You have something we can wear? I'm not sure I want to look like a missing member of the Village People."

Niall laughed, relieved to note the act didn't send pain spiraling through his head. He wasn't sure if the extra aspirin or the nap was the reason, but he was grateful either way. His headache had receded to a manageable dull throb, and he felt like he was thinking clearly again.

"Sure." Niall scooted to the edge of the mattress, planting his feet carefully on the floor and standing slowly. No head rush. Excellent, he thought, making his way across the small space so he could rummage through the bureau to find something suitable for them to wear.

He only kept T-shirts and shorts on the boat, but he managed to find enough clean and reasonably presentable clothes to dress both of them. It surprised him how much he liked the look of his much-beloved Humber Yawl Club shirt on Ethan. The cotton had been washed to the point of being threadbare, making it one of the softest shirts Niall owned. The frayed hem that looked messy on Niall managed to look adorable on Ethan, especially paired with the well-worn borrowed cargo shorts that hung low on his hips. Although Niall kept himself fit, Ethan was definitely thinner. Niall let his eyes wander appreciatively over the slice of tanned skin the low-slung shorts bared.

The boat rocked with the force of a swell, making Niall shake his head ruefully. He wondered if he'd ever have the opportunity to get Ethan naked when they weren't in the middle of a natural disaster.

When they were both dressed and outfitted in the life jackets once more, Niall decided to brave a look aboveboard. He could hear the wind had started to kick up again, but it didn't sound like it was raining again yet. The air was cool when he ducked his head up onto the deck, and he could see a few stars in the breaks in the clouds. He clambered up, with Ethan right behind him, and scrambled over to check the anchors. The nylon ropes looked a little frayed but would definitely hold up, assuming the tail end of Thalia wasn't more violent than the initial onslaught had been.

Squinting into the darkness, Niall scanned the cove, counting the other boats. It looked like all the boats that had been there when they'd dropped anchor were still there, and he counted two new ones as well. He hoped everyone was faring well aboard them.

Niall jolted when he felt Ethan wrap his arms around his waist, encumbered by the life vest but still close enough to make Niall's skin prickle with awareness. Ethan pressed a chaste kiss against the exposed skin of Niall's neck and Niall tilted his head to the side, staring out into the darkness past the mouth of the cove as he leaned back, an appreciative sound slipping past his lips.

"Head better?" Ethan's voice was slightly rough, which made Niall's stomach leap.

"Much."

Ethan nipped at Niall's earlobe, making Niall shiver involuntarily. The answering chuckle vibrated against his ear, making Niall swallow hard past the growing dryness in his throat. He hissed when sea spray coated them, the water cold against his face.

"I think that's our cue to get back below," Ethan whispered, the words just barely louder than the wind.

SIX

THINGS COULD, Niall reasoned, get worse. Things could always get worse. He looked up from the book he'd been reading, focusing on the television that was on across the room. The electricity was still on, thank God, and the weather channel was showing the radar on a constant loop, the blotchy swirls of brightly colored reds and greens superimposed above a satellite map of the island. The worst of Thalia had passed, but the island would probably be plagued by rain and high winds for days afterward.

When Niall had sold virtually all of his possessions and moved to the island, he hadn't thought about practical things, like the fact that the quaint little bungalow would need to be boarded up several times a season. He'd been too lost in the grief of Nolan's death and the secret thrill of making such a huge life change to care about the insanely high insurance premiums or that the tidy sum he'd made off selling his townhouse was little more than a meager down payment on the Orion. He'd even given up his dog, since bringing Laertes with him would have been more hassle than he or the eight-year-old golden retriever could withstand. Camille had been beside herself at the prospect of giving Laertes a home, though it was a kindness it would take Niall years to repay, especially since Stephanie hated dogs.

Now, though, with a hurricane winding down outside and another immovable force of nature—Ethan in full CEO mode—inside, Niall was beginning to wonder if the hard work necessary to keep his agency and the aforementioned quaint bungalow was worth it.

Ethan had set up camp at the kitchen table the minute they'd gotten back, spreading an astounding amount of paperwork across the scrubbed pine, followed by his laptop, a portable printer, and the phone he'd nearly thrown overboard the night before when he'd realized he didn't have service.

They'd slept for a few hours after the worst of Thalia had passed, roused by the Coast Guard when officers had hailed the Orion to make sure they were alright. Things had been a little strained since they'd returned to Tortola, which Niall blamed himself for. He'd been skittish when they'd woken up curled around each other for the second time, pulling away when Ethan had started to kiss him.

Niall wasn't sure how to explain his hesitancy to Ethan, but he knew he needed to find a way to make him understand that while he definitely was interested, things were moving too fast. Niall hadn't felt the slightest bit of attraction to anyone since Nolan's death, and he wasn't dealing well with the sudden return of his libido.

Ethan hadn't tried to touch Niall since they'd settled the Orion into her berth on Tortola and driven back to Niall's house. And while Niall was glad Ethan was giving him space, he knew it was for the wrong reasons. Ethan was cool and polite, nothing like the tender, funny man he'd been the night before. Niall had obviously hurt him when he'd pulled away, but he wasn't sure how to fix things. Niall knew he needed to tell Ethan about Nolan and that he hadn't been with anyone in the last four years, but it wasn't an easy conversation to start.

Niall looked over toward the boarded window near his chair, cocking his head to listen to the wind howl as it blew through the trees. He was incredibly grateful to his neighbors for securing his house while he'd been gone. Nolan had paid a caretaker a small fee to watch over the bungalow after he'd bought it, but Niall had taken over all those duties when he'd moved to the island. It was pure luck Mrs. Jim had noticed Niall's Jeep was missing from the carport and had the neighborhood boys who boarded up her windows do the same for his.

Niall's stomach grumbled and he belatedly remembered the shepherd's pie Mama Rosio had pressed on Ethan yesterday. They'd been in such a hurry to get the boat docked and themselves on dry land, they hadn't thought to grab it. He and Ethan hadn't eaten since dinner the night before, aside from the peanut butter crackers they'd scrounged out of the galley after the Coast Guard had roused them that morning.

Ethan was wrapped up in a conference call in the kitchen, so Niall gave him a wide berth as he walked around the table. Niall almost groaned out loud in frustration when he opened the refrigerator and realized the sole inhabitants were half a lime and a six-pack of Guinness. Luckily, a search of the freezer turned up a freezer-burnt pizza of unknown vintage, which Niall figured would have to be good enough. He didn't want to risk driving into town to get food. Even if they did, he doubted the restaurants would be open. Most of the businesses on the island shut down during bad storms, with the exception of a few of the smaller restaurants and bars where the owners lived upstairs. Those were dives even by Niall's low standards, and he couldn't imagine taking Ethan to one of them; frozen pizza was likely what they'd get there, anyway, but it would probably be of even more dubious origin than the one in Niall's hands.

The kitchen was small—the entire bungalow was small—and Niall could reach most of the appliances from the center of the room. Before he could flick the oven on, the lights flickered and dimmed, holding on for several long seconds before going out. Niall had been expecting it; in fact, he'd been surprised to come back and find the power still on at all. It wasn't uncommon for trees uprooted during a storm to fall a few hours afterward in the gusty winds that followed, taking out any power lines that hadn't been taken out by the storm itself.

"Shit."

"Generator?" Ethan's tone wasn't the slightest bit hopeful.

"No, I'm afraid not."

Ethan sighed, his face lit by his laptop screen. It seemed abnormally bright in the otherwise darkened room. The boards on the windows were far enough apart to allow a few slivers of sun to shine inside, though the clouds and rain obscured most of it anyway.

Niall jumped when he heard the front door open, momentarily cursing himself for not reinforcing it from the inside. The year before, Hurricane Igor had blown it open, splintering the wood and ruining most of his living room furniture when it let the lashing rain in. A thin beam of bright light cut through the gloom, followed by the sound of footsteps on the wood floor.

"Niall?"

"Mrs. Jim?" Niall hurried out into the living room in time to see the elderly woman shake the rain off her parka hood and draw it back, her gray hair knotted into its familiar tight bun.

"I saw you had a guest, and I didn't like to think of the two of you going hungry." It took Niall's eyes a moment to adjust to the darkness enough to see the box she held in her arms. He stepped forward automatically to take it from her. She was upwards of eighty and strong as an ox, but he always looked out for her, doing things like carrying her groceries in and mowing the meager patch of grass her house sat on.

"You didn't have to do that, Mrs. Jim," he said, his stomach growling traitorously at the scents wafting out of the box.

The older woman studied Niall shrewdly, shining the beam of her flashlight over the bandage on his head. She clucked her tongue, pulling out a kitchen chair and waiting expectantly. He sank into it, leaning his head forward without needing to be told so she could inspect the cut. Her arthritic fingers were gentle as she peeled the bandage back, tutting when he hissed as his hair got caught in the tape.

"I had a feeling you'd done something foolish like spending the night on that boat." The words were full of reprimand, but her touch was still gentle as she held the bandage back.

"Brilliant deduction." It was the first time Ethan had spoken since Mrs. Jim had arrived, and Niall cringed a bit at the condescending tone. Apparently Ethan's bad mood wasn't only aimed at Niall.

Mrs. Jim's lips twitched at the words, and Niall grinned.

"Don't know about brilliant. More just common sense," she drawled, swinging the beam of the flashlight over to the table where Ethan still sat, illuminated by his computer screen. "Lights weren't on here all night and Niall is fonder of that damn fool boat than just anything else in this world." She gave Niall another stern look. "And since I happen to know both Camille and his dog are safely out of danger, I figured it had to be the boat."

She stepped back from Niall, rummaging in the big pocket of the parka for something while she continued talking.

"I'd have called you, Niall, but by the time I got word they were upgrading it just about everyone knew." She cast a look at Ethan, whose lips were curled into a frown. "My son works at the NOAA hurricane center in Florida."

Ethan looked over at his phone, which was buried under a pile of files near his computer.

"My brother—"

"Your brother Aaron works with my Philip," she said, nodding when Ethan's eyes narrowed. "I know who you are, Mr. Bettencourt. Even if you weren't in a fair number of the magazines at the grocery checkout, I'd recognize you from the photo they put in the annual report prospectus."

"You—"

Mrs. Jim seemed determined not to let Ethan finish a sentence, which Niall found endearing. Ethan had been pulling the rug out from under him ever since he arrived on Tortola, and it was nice to see the tables turned a bit. Her soft Southern accent often threw people off; there was definitely more than a hint of steel running through Mrs. Jim.

"I'm a stockholder, yes. Oh, don't try to place the name. I only own about 100,000 shares."

Ethan seemed flabbergasted.

"Curse it, I didn't bring my kit." She pursed her lips, casting a critical eye over the gash on Niall's temple. "You boys eat that while it's hot. Took the roast out of the oven just before the power went out. The bread's from RiteWay, but you can't have everything. There's some canned food in the bottom of the box, Niall. I didn't figure you'd replenished your stores after the last one."

Niall shook his head, chagrined.

"I'll be back in a second," she said, pulling the hood of her parka back up. Niall craned his neck to try to peer through the cracks in the boards. It must be raining. "Be sure to run some water out, you hear? If you don't have jugs for it, you can just fill the bathtub. You don't want to be without."

It happened less often than losing power, but Niall could remember several times in the few years he'd lived here when they'd lost that too. He was already cursing himself for not thinking about it. He hadn't been himself since they'd gotten back, and it had nothing to do with the head injury Mrs. Jim was so worried about.

"I'm fine," Niall said, grabbing one of Mrs. Jim's hands and holding her there.

"You need stitches. Probably told the Coast Guard you'd see a doctor on land, I imagine." Niall flushed guiltily. Mrs. Jim hummed in annoyance. "Like I said, I'll be right back."

Niall stood and walked her to the door, but she brushed aside his concern that she shouldn't be out in the rain. He'd offered to come with her, but that had been met with an even stauncher rebuke. Not wanting to draw more of Mrs. Jim's wrath, Niall ducked into the spare closet in the hallway, where he kept his hurricane supplies. He grabbed half a dozen large pitchers to store water. The bathroom was the closest tap to the closet, plus it had the added benefit of being out of Ethan's warpath, so Niall took the pitchers in there and began the slow process of filling them. He left them where they sat and returned to the closet, perplexed when he couldn't find the battery operated lanterns and the candles he knew he'd bought.

He could hear Ethan murmuring in the other room, but since he hadn't heard the front door open, Niall figured Ethan was probably on the phone and not verbally abusing Mrs. Jim again. Niall couldn't understand why Ethan seemed to have taken an instant dislike to the woman.

Niall crowed in triumph when he found the lanterns under the sink in the bathroom. He'd probably put them there after the last bad storm, thinking it would be easier for him to find. Clearly, that had been a miscalculation. The box of candles and matches were there, too, but he was reluctant to get them out. Candlelight might only make things worse between himself and Ethan; namely, making Ethan look even more outrageously attractive and lowering Niall's already tenuous grasp on his self-control. Ethan had made it pretty clear since their return that he wasn't interested in taking things any further, and though it left Niall confused and a bit hurt, he respected that. All in all, Ethan was probably saving him from making a huge mistake. He was already too emotionally invested to have a one-night stand, which was apparently all Ethan wanted.

Ethan had already sorted through the box by the time Niall finished with the water. Canned vegetables and stews were stacked on one of the chairs, and Ethan had cleared enough space on the table to make room for two generously sized sandwiches that looked like they were stuffed with roast pork and an enormous thermos of what Niall assumed was soup.

"Dorothy Jimison." Ethan looked supremely proud of himself.

Niall grinned, placing the lantern at the center of the table and fiddling with it until it lit up, cutting through the gloom and lighting a fair amount of the kitchen.

"Why do you call her Mrs. Jim?"

Niall paused, the plates and bowls he'd gathered from the cupboard in his hands.

"She doesn't like the formality of Mrs. Jimison, and I didn't feel right calling her Dorothy," Niall said with a shrug. He set his burden on top of a pile of file folders, ignoring the way the bowls tipped a bit to the side as he poured hot soup into them from the thermos. "Mrs. Jim seemed as good a choice as any."

Ethan nodded, saving one of the bowls when it started to slide off the haphazard pile. He stacked it onto a plate, tucking half of one of the enormous sandwiches onto the side and holding both in his lap as he sat back.

"Get through to your brother?"

"It's entirely possible I remembered her name all on my own," Ethan said, his mock affront ruined by his lips twitching. "Okay, yes. I called Aaron. He does work with her son. It turns out Philip is actually the director of the center. And she was right about Thalia still causing trouble. He said there's more wind and rain in store today and tonight, but I should be clear for takeoff tomorrow morning."

The words hit Niall like a punch in the gut. He'd known Ethan was anxious to get home. He'd only planned to be away two days, after all, and he'd been working like a fiend ever since they'd gotten back to the bungalow, but he was still unprepared to hear Ethan talk about flying home as though it was nothing.

"I doubt the runways will be back in business by then."

"I called my pilot. He'll have the plane ready. The commercial runways are still full of debris, but the smaller ones are alright."

Niall snapped his mouth closed, jaw set in a tight line as he finished distributing lanterns around the living room. He didn't want to take the boards off the windows until all of the high winds had passed; he'd learned that lesson the hard way a year earlier when a tree had come through his front window.

He heard a perfunctory knock on the door before it opened, admitting Mrs. Jim and a swath of sunlight. Her parka was mostly dry this time, which must mean there had been another lull in the storm. Niall was tempted to go outside and start cleaning up debris around his property, but he knew Mrs. Jim wouldn't allow that. Not until she'd gotten her hands on him, at least.

"Ah, you got the lanterns out. Good. Hard enough to sew straight with these old eyes in the light, let alone the dark."

Ethan stared at her, aghast. His jaw dropped when Niall folded himself back into the chair, flipping it around so he could rest his chin on the back, allowing Mrs. Jim unfettered access to him from the side. She reached into the large case she'd brought in, washing her hands with a sanitizer that was strong enough to make Niall's eyes water before snapping on a pair of rubber gloves.

"Surely you don't intend to let her sew you up?"

Niall shrugged. When he'd told the Coast Guard he'd see his doctor on the island, he'd had Mrs. Jim in mind, anyway. The hospitals would be clogged with people with worse injuries, and most of the private practice doctors would be there, helping out in the overcrowded ER.

"I call her Mrs. Jim," Niall said, arching an eyebrow at Ethan when he opened his mouth to interrupt. "But most of the town calls her Dr. Dorothy. She came here, what, about twenty years ago?" Mrs. Jim nodded absently, scrutinizing the supplies she'd lined up on the sterile pad she'd laid over the table. Niall hissed when she rubbed something cool into his cut, but the sting was quickly replaced by a spreading numbness.

"Anyway, she came here about twenty years ago as part of a relief mission after a Cat 4 hurricane. She liked it so much she stayed."

"That's the abridged version, at least," she said, poking at the edges of Niall's gash with a needle. "Feel that?"

He winced, but shook his head as much as he dared with something so sharp that close to his scalp.

"Just pressure, really. A little sting."

"What have you taken?"

"Aspirin. I'm probably due for another dose."

She looked over at Ethan, who was still staring at them in disbelief. "I have some prescription-strength Tylenol in there. Have to have Philip send it to me because they don't sell it here," she said, rolling her eyes for Niall's benefit. "Be a love and find it for me, will you? And get Niall a glass of water. He'll want to take those as soon as I'm done. This'll ache something fierce when the numbing agent wears off."

She bent over Niall's head, stitching up the gash with a competency that obviously surprised Ethan, from the way he was gaping at them. Niall held back a chuckle, trying hard to stay still as Mrs. Jim stitched him up. As tired and woozy as he was, he could still appreciate how out of his depth Ethan seemed to be. As he watched Ethan give Mrs. Jim a considering look before he headed off to grab what she'd asked him to find, Niall was confident Ethan would be plotting how to get back on an even keel with her. In the short time he'd known him, Niall knew one of the things Ethan couldn't stand was being underestimated—he imagined that went both ways. Ethan had really gotten off on the wrong foot with Dr. Dorothy Jimison, but Niall knew Ethan would find some way to set that to rights. Besides, Mrs. Jim didn't hold grudges, but that wasn't something he was inclined to share with Ethan. He was having too much fun watching him be flustered.

SEVEN

THERE WASN'T much in Niall's living room to read that wasn't about boating, aside from a few real estate trade magazines that held even less interest for him at the moment. He didn't have much time to spare, and when he did, he often found himself down at the local bar or out at the beach instead of holed up at home reading.

He looked at the mess of glossy magazines haphazardly arranged on the table, all of them featuring pictures of striking sailboats on calm seas and gorgeously appointed yachts and plenty of smiling, tanned models to complement them.

Nolan had been the boat enthusiast, not Niall. Nolan had always coveted yachting catalogs, hiding them under his mattress and stuffing them in between the pages of his math books the same way other boys did skin magazines. For Niall the thrill had been getting out there on the boat—any boat—but Nolan had an appreciation for the artistry it took to craft a beautiful vessel.

Niall flipped through the magazine in his lap. He'd started subscribing to the bevy of catalogs and yachting magazines currently strewn all over his coffee table after he and Nolan had started dating, but he hadn't opened one until after Nolan's death. He'd simply kept a pile of them, sticking them in an envelope and mailing them off to whatever far-flung location where Nolan was stationed. It had been one of the only comforts Niall could offer him, aside from the knowledge that when Nolan came home, he'd be there waiting for him. And he had been—through the long, lonely years in the Royal Marines until Nolan had gotten his discharge, and then afterward, when Nolan had moved into his townhouse and they'd had their two blissful years of normal life until Nolan's sudden death.

Niall blinked back unexpected tears, immediately dismissing them as a symptom of his concussion. Part of him knew the reason he was thinking of Nolan so much was because of his feelings for Ethan. It felt almost disloyal to Nolan, though Niall knew Nolan wouldn't begrudge him falling in love again.

Falling in love, where did that thought come from, Niall wondered? He was being ridiculous. He hardly knew Ethan, and the man was leaving in the morning. Niall sighed, forcing himself to relax back into the pillows. He had agreed to take it easy, which ended up not being an empty promise after Ethan and Mrs. Jim had joined forces, apparently becoming fast friends after Ethan apologized for his boorish behavior and then asked for her roast recipe. Thoughts about his dead lover and his as-of-yet-uncategorized feelings for his client were definitely not doing his blood pressure or his headache any favors.

They'd been able to cajole Mrs. Jim into staying to eat lunch with them, but she'd left afterward, saying she planned to head down to the clinic to see if she could be of any assistance. Ethan offered to drive her, and to Niall's surprise, she accepted his offer. That had been two hours ago, and Ethan still wasn't back.

Niall was tense as he reclined on the couch, his worry ratcheting up with every minute that passed and Ethan didn't return. He felt the same heavy guilt he'd experienced the night before swamping over him. Ethan didn't know the island. He wasn't familiar with Niall's Jeep. The weather was too unpredictable, the wind too dangerous. And God only knew what the state of the roads was. Ethan could have run into a tree or a downed power line. He could have—

Niall heard the crunch of tires on the gravel outside and let out a breath he hadn't known he'd been holding. Ethan was back. And he'd better have a damned good explanation of why it had taken him two hours to take Mrs. Jim to the clinic, which was only five minutes away on a good day.

"Where have you been?" Niall winced as the words left his mouth. He hadn't meant to sound quite so much like an angry fishwife.

"I stopped by the airport on my way back to check on my plane." The expression on Niall's face was thunderous, so Ethan hurried to explain. "The roads really aren't bad at all, and your friend Jacks was at the hospital—no, he's fine, he'd brought his neighbor in—and he told me the road was clear all the way over. My pilot had said the wind had been particularly bad over there last night, so I thought I'd go see if the plane had been damaged."

Niall arched an eyebrow, but the motion hurt his scalp, deepening his frown.

"All set for takeoff tomorrow, don't worry."

"Don't worry?"

Ethan shrugged. "I need to get back, Gilligan, and I figure you'll be happy to get me out of your hair."

"I think I'd be the Skipper in that instance. You'd be Gilligan."

Ethan laughed. "I'd be the Professor if I was anyone. But fair enough, I'll give you the Skipper."

"You're not putting me out by being here, Ethan. Hurricane aside, I've enjoyed having you here."

Ethan seemed to hesitate, but then waved off Niall's protest as if he hadn't spoken.

"I've got some more work to do before I go back to pick Mrs. Jim up in a few hours," he said, disappearing into the kitchen without another word.

"I'm sure you're very busy. Coconut phones don't make themselves," Niall muttered as he focused on his magazine, glaring a hole in the picture of a carefree couple aboard a ridiculously large yacht.

He looked over his shoulder to see if Ethan had heard him, but Ethan was already absorbed in a phone call, his Blackberry pinched between his shoulder and ear as he typed furiously on his laptop. Niall sighed, leaning back on the pillows, and picking up his magazine again. The medication Mrs. Jim had given him had lowered his headache to manageable levels, and without the pain to distract him, Niall found himself nodding off to sleep.

THE FIRST thing Niall noticed when he woke was that he was blisteringly hot, which made no sense. He'd been dreaming about sailing—not the lazy type the tourists did on the islands, but the exhilarating, often freezing, type he used to do with Nolan back home in Hull. Niall's father had taken them both under his wing and taught them the ropes, and by the time they were teenagers, he and Nolan had become a constant presence around Humber Yawl, the sailing club Niall's father belonged to. They'd helped out with all of the mundane chores that went into boat upkeep and generally made themselves invaluable around the docks. It had paid off; they'd crewed for some of the fastest boats out there over their summer breaks during secondary school.

So when Niall woke from a dream about the icy spray of the North Sea, he was disoriented to find he was sweating. He opened his eyes, groaning as his head throbbed, and blinked at the murky twilight. Which couldn't be right, because he'd boarded the windows.

Niall shot up, dislodging the blanket that had made him so hot as he slept, and scrambled to his feet. The sky outside was clear but darkening. Someone had taken the boards off his windows. The house was quiet, but Ethan had mentioned going to pick Mrs. Jim up, so Niall assumed that was where he'd gone. After unboarding his windows, apparently. Niall was oddly touched by the gesture.

He flicked the switch in the kitchen, wrinkling his nose when the light failed to come on. Someone must have given the all clear on the wind if Ethan had taken down the storm shutters, but apparently the power company hadn't been able to fix the downed lines yet. He tried the kitchen faucet to see, relieved when water filled the sink. Even with the pitchers he'd drawn earlier, living without running water was a pain. The water heater was out, which meant no way to heat the water for a shower, but Niall had always found cold showers preferable to no showers.

He'd be especially grateful for it later if Ethan remained aloof, Niall thought sourly. He wasn't sure how to broach the subject with Ethan, but Niall definitely wanted to continue what they'd started last night. Even knowing he was probably setting himself up for a one-night stand, Niall had come to the decision that he still wanted to pursue things with Ethan. He knew he'd hurt Ethan when he'd been startled by Ethan's casual affection earlier, but he'd make it up to him when Ethan got back. Headache aside, Niall hadn't felt this sexually frustrated since he was a teenager.

Niall glanced at his watch. It was after 6:00 p.m., which explained the darkening twilight outside. The clinic usually closed by 7:00 p.m., but he doubted it would turn anyone away tonight, which meant Mrs. Jim might be out late, and Ethan with her. His stomach grumbled, and Niall poked around the kitchen until he found the box of supplies Mrs. Jim had brought over earlier. Despite having a gas range, he couldn't use it because it required electricity to run. There was an old camp stove out in the shed where he kept his fishing gear, though, and Niall headed outside, grabbing one of the battery powered lanterns on his way out.

He paused on the porch, frowning as he noticed his Jeep in the driveway. He could also see dim lights through Mrs. Jim's windows across the yard, probably from lanterns like the one he was holding. Niall set it down on the porch railing and sprinted across the still-wet grass to his neighbor's, slipping and sliding since he had no shoes on.

"Niall! Is your headache worse? Ethan said you were sleeping, or I would have checked in on you when we got back." Mrs. Jim opened her screen door, letting Niall pass into her foyer. The scrubbed pine floors were smooth beneath his bare feet, and he looked down at his dirty toes with embarrassment. She lived in a large plantation-style home that was much nicer than his own house. Niall figured the bungalow had probably once been servants' quarters.

"He should have woken me when you got back. He must be starving." Niall tried not to be obvious about looking for Ethan, his eyes darting past Mrs. Jim into the dark hallway behind her. He couldn't see any sign of him.

Mrs. Jim pursed her lips, fixing Niall with a stern look that didn't seem to have any heat behind it, as though she was angry with someone else.

"I told Ethan you'd be upset if he left without saying goodbye." Niall's jaw hardened at her words, and her demeanor instantly softened. "He asked me to tell you he'd call you in a few days. Ethan's pilot, Joe—he was an Army medic, did you know that?—was helping me at the clinic when we got word of a woman over on Virgin Gorda who needed more medical attention than she could get there. He and Ethan flew over to get her, figuring that would be faster since all the runways are cleared but the docks are still a mess."

Niall nodded. Ethan had already told him the airport on Tortola was fine, and it wasn't surprising the same was true on Virgin Gorda. They kept the airports free of trees and smaller structures for a reason.

"Well, by the time they got there, the doctor was recommending she be taken to the States by Medevac. She was a tourist from Florida," she said with an eye roll, and Niall snorted. Tourists almost always insisted they be taken home for treatment, since they worried the island hospitals were too backwater. The doctors usually signed off on the transfer, as long as the patient was stable enough to be moved and their insurance agreed.

"Let me guess. Ethan and his pilot offered to fly her to Miami?"

Mrs. Jim nodded and Niall relaxed. It was a three-hour flight, and it would probably take a few hours to get the woman to the hospital and refuel. At worst, Ethan would spend the night there and be back in the morning.

"He said he had everything he needed either on board the plane already or at the clinic with him, since he'd been using the hospital's generator to power his computer."

Niall's heart sank. He kept his smile in place, leaning in to press a quick kiss to her cheek.

"Thanks, Mrs. Jim."

"Oh now, Niall, don't be angry with him. I'm sure he'll explain when he calls."

Niall nodded, his head throbbing.

"Of course," he said, giving her a little wave before picking his way back through the debris that cluttered their joined yards. He could tell Mrs. Jim wholeheartedly believed Ethan was going to call, and he wanted to believe it, but he just couldn't.

EIGHT

"YOU'RE ABSOLUTELY right. It is a lovely property, which is why Maxine and Earl Alexander submitted an offer this morning." Niall slid a file folder out from underneath a half-full mug, biting back an oath when it, predictably, tipped and splashed both his desk and his lap with thankfully tepid coffee.

"No, I don't think it was an unreasonable offer." Niall rolled his eyes as the woman on the other end of the phone—the estate agent for the seller—launched into a high-pitched tirade about the insultingly low offer. Niall personally agreed with her and had advised the Alexanders against making such a low-ball opening bid for the small, ranch-style home on the north side of the island. The real estate market was a bit pinched in Tortola and across the rest of the cluster of islands, but not so much so that an offer of more than $100,000 under the asking price was reasonable.

"Yes, I realize comparable homes in the area have sold for much more," Niall said, wheeling his office chair back and ransacking his filing cabinet for something to soak up the mess the coffee had made. The receiver nearly jerked out of his hand as he reached the end of his cord, and he gritted his teeth, wheeling back to the desk. He was about to use the wadded-up Kleenex he'd found in his desk drawer when a pile of paper towels dropped into his line of vision. He looked up, mouthing a silent thank you to Keandra.

"I disagree. Dismissing the offer outright is what's unreasonable." Niall fought the urge to sigh when the woman started to squawk at his tone. "I'm not saying that. I'm saying my clients are expecting a counteroffer. That's how the game is played."

The papers on his desk were a lost cause, so Niall picked up the dripping mess and dropped it into the wastebasket, mentally noting he'd need to have Keandra print new copies before his showing later that afternoon.

"No, I'm not saying you don't know how to do your job." Niall pinched the bridge of his nose, willing away the headache that was building. He'd been having them with increasing frequency since Thalia blew through three weeks earlier, but despite Mrs. Jim's growing concern, he refused to get it checked out at the hospital. He already knew the cause, and he knew he deserved to have his head examined—by a different sort of doctor—for allowing the mysterious Ethan Bettencourt's whirlwind weekend on the island and subsequent departure to affect him. The headaches were stress, pure and simple. Niall firmly insisted to himself the headaches were brought on by the loss of the income that would have come from selling a house to Ethan and not in any way due to Ethan leaving so abruptly and not returning any of the calls Niall had made to his office afterward.

It was ridiculous to miss a man he'd known for less than forty-eight hours. Niall refused to let himself wallow. He'd thrown himself with renewed vigor into saving his business. The fact that Ethan had turned out to be a bastard didn't change Niall's plans to sell the agency and pay off the Orion's mortgage; it just made it a little more difficult.

"I will definitely take that to them," Niall said into the receiver, scribbling the counteroffer down on a Post-it pad that had somehow escaped the deluge of coffee. "No, I agree it's a fair counter. I'll meet with the Alexanders and get back to you as soon as they make a decision."

He exchanged a few pleasantries with the shrill-voiced agent, absently doodling on the edges of the Post-it as they fell into typical

island chat about how things had been faring since the hurricane—
which shops had been damaged, whose roof blew off, whose dog
was still lost. It was a conversation he'd had dozens of times in the
last few weeks, until she mentioned a new client in her office.

"He was on the island for the hurricane, can you imagine? A
big-shot client like that and the agent he was meeting with didn't
think to check the tropical storm forecast before having him come
out."

Niall's mouth went dry, and he blinked when he realized he'd
absently written the word "Ethan" on his Post-it. He scratched it out,
then tore off the sheet and tossed it into the trash for good measure,
retrieving it a second later to copy the counteroffer off of it onto a
fresh one.

"Really? So he switched agencies afterward?"

"Of course he did. Wouldn't you? If that's the kind of
competence you can expect from an agent, it hardly inspires
confidence, does it?" Niall hummed in agreement, afraid of speaking
in case she realized how interested he was in her idle office gossip.

Was that why he hadn't heard from Ethan? He didn't want to
believe Ethan could do something so harsh and calculating, but Niall
had to admit to himself that at his core, Ethan was a businessman.
And if he'd been unhappy with Niall's performance, Niall had no
doubt Ethan would have jumped ship to a different office. But not to
tell him about it? To ignore the four personal messages Niall had left
for him and have his secretary return the business calls? He didn't
think Ethan was that cold. Then again, Ethan had left without a
word, so maybe he was.

What if it hadn't been Niall's real estate agent services that
had sent Ethan running? What if it had been him? Ethan had seemed
plenty interested, but he'd certainly backed off quickly.

"—she apparently hadn't even booked him a hotel for his stay.
This is a client looking at multimillion-dollar homes and the agent
doesn't book him a hotel. His wife was furious. Furious. And then to

be on the island during a hurricane—it's amazing they're still interested in buying property in Tortola."

Niall had only been half listening, but the tail end of her story caught his attention.

"His wife? The client is married?"

"Well, sure. Most of them are. Though we had someone in here last year who wanted us to help him find a place to shack up with his mistress. He even admitted that's what it was for! I couldn't believe it. Of course, we made the sale. Money's money, right?"

Niall's temples were throbbing and he pulled a bottle of ibuprofen out of his drawer. He'd had Keandra pick it up for him last week, and now it was nearly empty. He'd have to do something about his headaches before all the medication he was taking for them ate a hole in his stomach. That or his worry over Ethan.

"Did the client tell the old agent he was dumping him?" Niall's stomach lurched a bit, though he wasn't sure if it was in response to swallowing the pills dry or the anxiety that Ethan might have abandoned him professionally as well as personally. Ethan's secretary had said he was busy with a software release for the next few weeks and couldn't come back to look at more property until November at the earliest, but what if that had just been Ethan's way of politely letting him down?

"Oh you bet he did." The agent was clearly enjoying relaying the juicy bit of gossip. "She's with Stark-Madison over on Virgin Gorda."

"She?" Niall's throat felt like sandpaper as he forced the word out. The other agent didn't notice, plowing ahead with her story.

"Not that she'll be with them much longer. I can't imagine Damon Stark not firing her on the spot—"

"That's, wow. Yeah. Thanks," Niall interrupted, his heart racing. "I'll get the counteroffer to the Alexanders. Nice talking to you, Becky."

He hung up before she had a chance to respond, not caring what she made of him abruptly ending the conversation. It hadn't struck Niall how much he was counting on seeing Ethan again until he'd thought he wouldn't be.

He tried to convince himself his interest in Ethan was purely professional, telling himself he was grateful Ethan left before they could do anything they'd both regret. But even though he knew it was pointless to dwell on it, he couldn't get the feel of Ethan's body cuddled up against his out of his mind. Memories of the taste of Ethan's mouth or the electric thrill of his stubble grazing against bare skin kept Niall up at night, and when he did manage to go to sleep, he'd find himself waking up with the phantom feel of Ethan's lips on his, aroused and alone.

Niall took a deep breath, pushing back from his desk. He'd call the Alexanders about the counteroffer—which he privately thought was a very good deal, but he knew the American couple wouldn't agree—from the car as he drove home to grab a change of clothes. He couldn't very well show a house in coffee-stained khakis.

NINE

NIALL WAS fairly sure the telephone had been invented, not by Alexander Graham Bell, but by the devil himself.

He'd been on the phone nonstop all day, relaying offers and counteroffers and stipulations for three different sales, but that wasn't what currently had him pacing a hole in his hallway, phone clenched so tightly in his fist it left grooves in his skin.

"There's been a mistake. I haven't paid the loan off. God, I wish I had. But I haven't."

There was silence on the other end of the phone, and Niall could hear the customer service representative typing furiously on his keyboard. Niall held his breath and counted to five, letting out a stream of air until he felt his lungs burn. He took a slow breath in, focusing on the feeling of his lungs refilling. Apparently it was an old relaxation technique that had been used in yoga for centuries. Stephanie had recommended he try it after telling him he sounded tense during their last phone conversation.

"I'm sorry, sir, but I do not show you having an active loan with First National. Your account shows the balance of $428,751.29 was paid in full two weeks ago."

Niall rested his head against the wall, blowing out another breath. Feeling silly as he did it, Niall followed the rest of

Stephanie's advice. He pictured all of his stress and frustration leaving his body on the long breath out, focusing on positive energy as he inhaled. It didn't help.

"But I did not make a payment of $400,000 and whatever the hell else you said. I made my normal monthly payment of $3,891 last week and came home today to a notice I'd overpaid my account."

There was more typing on the other end of the phone, and Niall nearly screamed with frustration.

"Yes, sir. I do show an electronic payment of $3,891 was logged on Monday. The system flagged the overpayment several hours after that, but the funds had already been transferred. Are you calling to check on the status of your refund check? The letter you received stated refunds are issued between ten to fourteen days after—"

Niall clenched his fist harder, fighting the urge to wing the phone across the room.

"I am not calling about a refund. I do not want my payment refunded. I want my payment credited to my account so I don't get another letter in two weeks about late fees I have incurred because my monthly loan payment was late."

The house seemed to ring with silence as Niall waited for the customer service representative to answer. His breathing sounded abnormally loud, and he realized he was sweating. Perhaps Stephanie had been right about his stress level.

"Sir, you have no monthly payment. You have no loan with First National." The man paused, obviously waiting for Niall to respond. When he didn't, the voice became more chipper. "Thank you for calling First National, your first choice for all your banking needs. If there is any other way I can be of assistance—"

"Other implies you were of assistance in the first place," Niall snarled, hitting the end button with much more force than necessary. He stalked into the living room, hurling the phone into the sofa cushions. It sank between two of them, disappearing into the folds.

He'd bought the boat in North Carolina and the loan had been from a bank in New Jersey, where he'd been staying with Stephanie. He hadn't shopped around or even taken a test drive before settling on the sleek forty-one-foot yacht. He'd have bought the Albemarle 410C sight unseen if the company had let him, but they'd refused to sell him the yacht without him actually coming out in person.

The boat had been Nolan's current favorite when he'd died, made by a family-owned company in North Carolina known for its quality construction and attention to detail. Nolan had known every inch of that boat by memory, so when he died and Niall sold most of his worldly goods to move to Nolan's home in Tortola, it had been the obvious choice. They'd planned to go into the charter business together after Niall had saved up money as an estate agent and Nolan came home for good from Afghanistan, but things hadn't gone according to plan. Niall figured if he had to fulfill their shared dream alone, he would do it with the boat Nolan had chosen, no matter how financially irresponsible it was.

He'd sold his townhouse in Hull for a tidy sum, but despite that he'd only had about $400,000, which hadn't been nearly enough to buy the boat and get the charter business up and running. The insurance premiums alone were astronomical, not to mention the actual cost of the yacht and its upkeep. So he'd put a $200,000 down payment on it and gotten a loan from First National for the rest, using Nolan's house in Tortola as collateral, since he'd technically been unemployed at the time.

Niall squeezed his eyes shut, wondering what to do next. He'd try the bank again in the morning and not let them off the phone until they let him talk to a manager. He'd demand they sort out his account and refuse to pay any late fees that might have been incurred because of the debacle. And then as soon as he got a chance, he'd see if he could transfer his loan somewhere else.

That settled, Niall grabbed a beer and kicked off his shoes, too tired to worry about cooking. Truth be told, he wasn't hungry anyway after his forty-minute go-round with the bank. He sank into the armchair near the door and propped his feet on the table, staring at the blank television screen.

Wallowing, that's what Mrs. Jim had called it. And just yesterday, Keandra had said something similar, although unlike his elderly neighbor, she wasn't quite as circumspect about it. Niall knew it must have been bad for the usually professional Keandra to voice an opinion about it. They rarely spoke about their private lives; the only reason he knew as much as he did about her son was because she was Jacks's niece and Jacks talked about Sebastian all the time. And the only reason he knew she worked a second job on the late shift at the bar at the marina was because he'd seen her there himself. They didn't talk about much outside of work, but apparently his funk over Ethan's abrupt departure and subsequent complete cold shoulder was encroaching on his ability to work, and Keandra had taken notice.

Niall took another slow sip of his beer. The creamy taste made his stomach roll a bit. He wiped at his mouth, almost expecting to find a mustache from the foam. He didn't even like Guinness, but it felt disloyal to Nolan to drink something else while sitting in Nolan's house. Vitamin G my ass, he thought with a scowl, glaring at the can.

He set the beer aside without reluctance when the phone rang and began fumbling in the couch cushions. He'd nearly given up hope of catching the caller—the one his mind was most definitely not hoping was Ethan, calling to prostrate himself at Niall's feet, apologies flowing for leaving and not contacting him earlier—when he closed his fingers around the hard plastic.

He answered it quickly, not bothering to check the caller ID for fear of the person hanging up.

"Long time no see, mate."

Niall's heart sank at the familiar Scottish brogue.

"You know how it goes," Niall said with forced casualness, willing away the lump in his throat. He must not have been able to keep all of the disappointment out of his voice, since Ian immediately picked up on it.

"Down in the dumps then, eh?" Ian Mackay had spent a few years in America before moving to the islands. Not long enough to lose his accent, but long enough to pick up the worst of American slang. Normally it amused Niall, but tonight it reminded him of Ethan. Not that it was unusual—everything reminded him of Ethan, though how that was possible he wasn't sure. Ethan had been and gone so quickly it was almost like he'd never been there, except for the aching in Niall's chest and the blanket in the guest room that smelled faintly of Ethan's woodsy scent. Niall had tucked it into the closet after Ethan had left so the cleaning woman wouldn't wash it when she'd stripped the bed.

Niall listened as Ian shared the latest idle gossip, rounding out the stilted conversation by asking Niall to come out on Romeo's Rowboat. Ian's invitation to go sailing was hardly out of the blue. He'd been trying to cajole Niall out onto the boat for more than a year, but Niall had always preferred to keep his interactions with the notorious Lothario on dry land—and in public. He enjoyed his friendship with Ian, but he had no desire to be another notch on his mast, so to speak. Niall didn't have many real friends on the island, and he worried that if Ian made a move and he refused, he might lose Ian's casual friendship.

Niall opened his mouth to decline, as he always did, but a glint of light from the coffee table caught his attention. Tiny beads of condensation were forming on the cool metal of his beer can, coalescing into bigger beads until the surface tension broke and they cascaded down the side. Niall watched a rivulet course down the smooth surface, wishing he was free to move like that. The rivulet picked up speed as it moved and Niall suddenly felt something tight inside him loosen. Sailing. He hadn't been on a proper sailboat since he'd left Hull.

Going for a good sail might be just what he needed to shake himself out of his funk.

"Sure, Ian," he heard himself say. Niall could almost imagine the look of comic surprise on Ian's face at his acceptance, but Ian was quick to recover and sort out the details. Sitting at home brooding about Ethan was a mistake, but Niall hoped he wasn't making an even bigger mistake by taking Ian up on his offer.

LESS THAN an hour later, Niall was manning the tiller stick of a sloop, steering the small craft toward the horizon. The setting sun cast its orange reflection on the water, making it look like the sea's surface was sparkling with a light of its own.

"Beautiful," Ian drawled.

The tall, sandy-haired man had grown up in Edinburgh and immigrated to the British Virgin Islands after coming into a sizable inheritance from his grandparents a few years earlier, giving up his career as an investment banker in favor of lounging in the Caribbean with a string of live-in lovers who never seemed to last from one season to the next. One of the reasons Niall had never taken Ian up on his generous offer to borrow the sloop—aside from the indignity of sailing on something called Romeo's Rowboat—was he had no interest in the strings that came attached to it. But Niall had been too tempted by the desire to cut through the waves the way he used to, back when his life had been simple and his biggest worry had been whether his parents would notice he'd left his homework undone in favor of taking out the boat with Nolan.

Niall took a deep breath, still staring out at the setting sun. As far as sunsets went, tonight's wasn't anywhere near the best he'd seen on the islands. The sky was clear, free of the clouds that sometimes streaked with vibrant color, lit through by the sun.

"Yeah, the sun just over the water is a sight I never get tired of," Niall said, knowing that was the expected response. In truth, they'd set sail during the sunset simply by a coincidence of timing; he hadn't decided he wanted to go sailing until it had been near twilight.

"I don't know about that, but your ass in those jeans is definitely more interesting than a ball of fire disappearing." Niall could hear the leer in Ian's voice, and he forced himself not to turn around. This had been a mistake.

"We should turn back. It'll be full-on dark in twenty minutes, and Romeo's Rowboat doesn't have running lights," Niall answered, pulling on the stick to start to slowly swing the boat around. The boat's owner was every bit as foppish as its namesake, and Niall was regretting taking Ian up on his offer. He should have known Ian would see it as an opportunity.

"I don't mind being out after dark, darling," Ian murmured. Niall finally did turn to face him, a look of incredulity on his face.

"You don't mind being out after dark in a boat that has no lights and no navigational equipment? So no one can see us coming, and we can't see where we are? Are you an idiot?"

Ian bristled and Niall bit his tongue, tamping down on his tirade. He hated boat owners like Ian, people who viewed them as toys that could be used however they wanted without regard to basic safety and common sense. It was dangerous enough being out in the boat at twilight, but once the sun fully set, they'd be practically invisible. The stretch of ocean they were on wasn't a high-traffic channel, but there were still a fair number of boats passing through. Anyone with any degree of sailing know-how and sense would be apprehensive to be out; instead, all Ian could think of was getting laid. Niall glowered at him, pulling the steering stick with a bit more force than necessary. Ian was walking toward him, closing in on him quickly despite the rocking of the boat as it turned. With any luck, he'll pitch overboard, Niall thought, and then felt instantly contrite. Hadn't he just been mentally berating Ian for being an idiot about boat safety? And here he was, wishing him bodily harm.

Niall tensed as he waited for Ian to descend on him, surprised when no unwanted touch or words came. He looked up, impressed to see Ian expertly adjusting the mast so the sails caught the slight wind, hastening them toward the marina. Maybe he'd been a bit quick in his dismissal of Ian's sailing skills; he was obviously comfortable on the sloop, which meant he'd taken it out for more than impressing his dates and sunbathing.

Relaxing, Niall turned back to his task, making gentle modifications as needed to steer them back toward land. They were close, within sight of the docks, when Ian approached. Niall felt his presence rather than seeing Ian, since he was focused on steering the sloop into its berth. He started with surprise when Ian perched on the seat next to him, their bodies pressed together from hip to knee because of the tight space.

Niall ignored him, concentrating on pulling the boat up into its slot with as much care as he could. He winced when the hull butted against the piling, the sloop bouncing back slightly and drifting back against it with a jolt, bringing the boat to a full stop. Deck hands seemed to appear almost instantly, stepping over onto the hull and starting to dock the boat. Niall personally thought that people who didn't maintain their own boats didn't deserve to own them, but Ian clearly disagreed. The marina he kept Romeo's Rowboat at was considerably nicer than the one Niall's yacht was moored at; the marina took full responsibility for maintenance, including tying off the boats.

Niall was watching the young deck hands deftly knotting the ropes around the pylon, remembering when he and Nolan had done similar jobs back in Hull. His distraction left him wholly unprepared when Ian made a move, and he jumped when he felt the warm press of lips against the side of his jaw.

Ignoring the way Niall stiffened, Ian scooted closer, bringing his arm up to wrap around Niall's shoulder, his fingers sliding into the soft hair at the nape of his neck. The caress was enough to snap Niall out of his shocked silence, and he barked out Ian's name, roughly pushing him away.

Ian shot him a coquettish look and dove back in, teeth nipping lightly against the curve of Niall's jaw.

"For God's sake, stop, Ian. You're making a fool of yourself," Niall sputtered, abruptly pushing Ian, who had half climbed into his lap, onto the sloop's floor.

Instead of being chagrined, Ian seemed to take Niall's rough treatment of him as encouragement. He sat up on his knees, running his hands up Niall's thighs. Niall batted ineffectually at his hands, turning to see if there was anyone on the dock who he could call out to. He wasn't afraid of Ian—Niall was fairly sure he'd outclass him in a fight if it came to that—but he didn't want to embarrass Ian in front of anyone. Ian raised an eyebrow as he looked over Niall's shoulder at the deck hands still working to secure Romeo's Rowboat.

"Don't worry about them, love. They're discreet." Ian pressed back against Niall, his hands seemingly everywhere at once as he ran them over Niall's torso and back down to tease at the waistband of Niall's jeans.

"Ian, for Christ's sake!" Niall stood, stepping awkwardly around Ian and up onto the dock. The men merely smirked at him, making Niall sure this scene wasn't unusual in the least. Of course, Niall doubted the objects of Ian's amorous intentions usually left; Ian had a reputation as a man who would shag just about anyone, but Niall had never heard of anyone who hadn't left his clutches satisfied.

Far from looking embarrassed, as Niall had feared, Ian grinned at him and stood, brushing dirt and salt off his trousers.

"Can't blame a bloke for trying. No hard feelings?"

Niall offered Ian a hand as he stepped over the hull and onto the dock, a relieved laugh making its way past his lips. He really did like Ian, aside from the fact that he was constantly trying to get into his pants. It didn't hurt that he had a fair number of friends who always seemed to be looking for property. He'd thrown several clients Niall's way, and Niall would hate to lose his referrals—or his friendship, which was a good one, whorish tendencies aside.

"No hard feelings," Niall agreed, squeezing their joined hands before dropping his arm to his side and sticking his hands into his pockets. "But try it again and I will put you overboard."

Ian laughed, clapping Niall on the back heartily as the two of them made their way down the dock to the parking lot.

"Duly noted. Next time I'll be sure to make my move on dry land."

"Ian." The word was a little more than an exasperated sigh.

"Just joking, pet." Niall grunted again at the endearment. Ian laughed. "It's too easy to rile you, mate. Really."

Ian walked him all the way to his car, but before Niall could close the door, Ian's palm gripped the top of the frame. Niall looked up, ready with a retort for the next pass Ian made, but was surprised to see a serious expression on his friend's normally smiling face.

"What's on your mind, Niall?"

Niall tried for a grin but knew he fell short, the tense lines around his mouth not quite disappearing as his lips curved upward.

"Not what's on yours, I'm sure."

Ian laughed but didn't relinquish his grip on the door.

"You haven't been yourself lately. Jacks said you haven't been to The Cab since it reopened after the storm, and when I ran into Keandra at the deli yesterday, she said you'd been poorly. Headaches, she said." Ian didn't add heartaches to the list of Niall's supposed woes, but Niall could see the compassion in his friend's face. His dalliance with Ethan wasn't common island gossip—his few friends were far too loyal for that—but it wasn't a secret either. Anyone who actually knew Niall would be able to put two and two together and realize his recent behavior wasn't solely due to a bump on the head and the potential loss of a huge client.

"Well, there you go. Can't mix alcohol and the pain relievers I've been popping for my headaches." The excuse sounded thin even to Niall's ears.

"Then instead of asking you out for a drink, let's go to your place and have some coffee."

Niall was overcome by the sudden urge to put his fist through something. Why was Ian pursuing him so doggedly when he'd made it clear he wasn't interested? Niall clenched the steering wheel, clamping his jaw together. He took a breath, stopping himself from snapping at Ian. In truth, this wasn't unexpected behavior. This was Ian's natural personality, flirty and aggressive. It normally didn't bother Niall because he knew it was mostly for show, though tonight's incident on the boat was starting to make him doubt that. No, his anger didn't stem from Ian's pursuit; it was because he wished the man standing outside his car door peering at him in concern was Ethan.

"Ian, I—"

"Oh, for God's sake, Niall," Ian muttered, rolling his eyes. "I'm not going to try to seduce you. I gave it a go and you weren't interested. It's over and done. Honestly, I thought you could use the distraction of a good shag, but it's obvious you need to talk more than you need that." He looked at Niall speculatively. "From me, at least."

Niall let his head fall forward onto the steering wheel. This wasn't happening. He'd wake up in a few minutes and find himself back on the Orion in the middle of the hurricane. This and the last few infuriating weeks would all have been some crazy concussion dream, and he'd still be curled up in Ethan's arms.

"That settles it," Ian said cheerfully, wrenching the door the rest of the way open and nudging Niall's thigh with his knee. Niall stared at him in absent horror as he realized he'd said that last bit out loud. "Budge over. I'm driving you home, you're making me coffee, and then we're starting at the beginning of the story that ended with your client in your bed."

Niall snapped his mouth shut, unbuckling his seat belt and scooting over. Ian knew him well enough to know his policy on dating clients, as well as his recent celibacy, and Niall could tell from the gleam in his eye that Ian was like a dog with a bone—or an investment banker with a good lead. It wasn't in his nature to let things go, and like an idiot, Niall had given Ian the opening he needed.

"Fine." Niall crossed his arms over his chest, knowing it was petulant but not caring. "But just to clarify, he was in my bed, but he was not in my bed."

Ian laughed, starting the engine and testing the brakes as he eased the Jeep out of the parking lot, familiarizing himself with the controls. It was full-on dark now, and Ian struggled for a moment with levers and knobs until Niall reached over and flicked the headlights on for him.

"Not for lack of trying, though, eh? Sit back and tell the love doctor all about it, pet."

Niall let his head slam against the headrest, welcoming the burst of pain as the motion made his headache explode.

TEN

SIX DAYS, seventeen phone calls, a ferry ride, and a plane trip later, Niall found himself in the lobby of First National Bank in Newark, New Jersey. Ian had used his old banking contacts to help him get an appointment to see the bank manager to sort out Niall's boat mortgage mix-up. Niall tried to look calm and in control as he tapped his feet against the tile floor, unconsciously drumming out the beat from the song that had been playing in the car on the way over, some horrifying pop tune his niece Camille had known every word to. She and Stephanie had dropped him off outside the enormous building twenty minutes ago, heading to a nearby mall to shop and wait for him to finish.

He'd lived in the States for more than six months after Nolan's death, taking up residence in Stephanie and her husband Roger's guest suite. Camille had been thrilled to have her uncle living above the garage, but Niall figured after the first few months, Stephanie had been less so. As a freelance graphic designer, she worked from home, and Niall knew his presence was disrupting her workday— and not only because he was sleeping in her studio. She was used to having her days to herself while Roger took the train in to work in the city and Camille was at school. Having Niall there, no matter how welcome his presence was, disrupted her schedule. She'd taken a few weeks off after Nolan's death, but her clients hadn't been able to wait indefinitely. Eventually, she'd started encouraging Niall to leave the comforting confines of the guest quarters and get back out into the world—in part out of concern for him, but also because she wanted to move her computer back into the guest suite's living room. Working in the kitchen of the main house was driving her to distraction.

The talk she'd had with him back then bore a striking similarity to the one she'd subjected him to last night. He'd been in Newark for three days already, doting on Camille and watching football—which the thoroughly Americanized Camille called soccer but Niall swore he never would—with Roger. Last night Stephanie had, bolstered by half a bottle of wine, confronted him and told him she thought he had the wrong end of the stick in regard to Ethan.

"He hasn't had a hold of his stick at all, from the sound of it," Roger had snickered, making Stephanie flush with more than wine as Niall glared at him. "And that's the long and the short of it, so to speak."

"So I should go out there and bugger him senseless, then leave?" The words had been incredulous, but Niall did have to admit there was merit to Roger's plan.

"No!" Stephanie had shouted, throwing her hands up in the air. "You go out there and talk to him, Niall. Tell him how hurt you were when he left. Forget this artifice of returning the money if Ethan was even the one to pay off the boat—"

"It's not artifice, and I was not hurt!" Niall had yelled. The conversation had come to an abrupt end when Camille, who had been woken by the shouting, made her way downstairs into the kitchen and demanded they make her some cocoa if they couldn't be quiet enough for her to sleep.

Niall scuffed his foot against the floor, remembering a time when he wore shoes like the wingtips he had on at the moment most of the time. Now he could go to work in sandals if he liked, but he'd kept all of his dress clothes. They took up an inordinate amount of space in the bungalow's tiny closet, though he'd shoved most of them into the guest room. Nolan had loved it when he'd dressed up. Even after he'd been discharged from the service and saw Niall day in and day out, he still preferred him in a suit. He used to say Niall dressed to the nines was the absolute antithesis of the combat fatigues he'd gotten so tired of seeing over the years, and he'd kept a picture of him in these very wingtips in his pocket. It had been in his wallet when Niall had picked up Nolan's things from the funeral home. Niall remembered being surprised Nolan still carried it, even at home.

"Mr. Ahern?"

Niall looked up, rising when he saw a woman in a trim tweed suit motioning for him to follow her. The click of their heels seemed loud in the lobby, and she didn't speak until they'd gotten into an elevator.

"I'm Stacy LeBlanc, vice president of consumer services for First National," she said, shifting the folder in her hands to the crook of her elbow so she could shake Niall's hand. "I went to Yale with Ian Mackay."

"Niall Ahern," he offered, suddenly feeling sheepish about his mission. He wondered exactly what the prim and neat Stacy LeBlanc would think of him once he explained why he was there. If the increasingly exasperated tone of every bank employee he'd already spoken with about his account was anything to go by, he'd be breaking through her polite exterior any minute now.

"I must say I was intrigued when Ian called. We don't often get clients coming in with complaints like yours," she said as the elevator doors chirped and opened, revealing a lushly carpeted waiting room with expensive-looking furniture and fixtures. Niall hadn't expected a bank to be quite so opulently turned out. Then again, he wasn't just at a bank, he was at the bank's corporate headquarters. When Ian had told Niall he could "make a few calls" and get him a meeting, Niall hadn't expected this.

The slit in the back of Stacy's skirt flipped as she turned the corner and Niall saw a brief flash of the lacy top of her thigh-highs. Suddenly Stacy LeBlanc, vice president of consumer services, didn't seem quite so staid. Niall wondered how exactly she knew Ian. Was he dealing with a former conquest? His collar felt a bit tight as Niall swallowed, growing increasingly uncomfortable.

"Would you like something to drink? We have water and coffee here, or I could send someone down for something else," Stacy offered as they made their way farther into the suite, pausing in front of a corner office with her name on the door.

"No, thank you." Niall's skin itched as he felt sweat break across his back, reminding him of the last time he'd worn this suit. It strengthened his resolve and was enough to get him past his awkwardness. He'd had a lot of time to think about exactly what had happened, and he had a sinking suspicion his account hadn't been paid off by a bank error. Whether or not Stacy was a notch on Ian's bedpost, she was in the position to help him, and he wasn't going to waste the opportunity because he was afraid Stacy might be an angry ex-girlfriend of Ian's.

Stacy smiled and held her hand out, directing him to a small sofa along the wall with a low coffee table in front of it. Niall waited until she'd perched on the edge of the cushions before taking a seat himself. She spread his file out on the table in front of them. From his vantage point, Niall could see it detailed his payment history and the terms of the loan.

"Everything is pretty straightforward," Stacy said, rifling through the small stack of papers and handing Niall a copy of the letter he'd gotten from the bank thanking him for paying off his balance. "I've been over the file several times, and I don't believe this was due to an error. Though we do appreciate your honesty and concern, Mr. Ahern."

Niall swallowed, nodding.

"Ian said I should be able to see the record of payment if I came in," he said, his tone almost apologetic.

Stacy nodded, handing him another sheet of paper. The avid interest in her gaze confirmed Niall's suspicions even before he had a chance to read the name on the account.

"Mr. Bettencourt authorized the transfer from his account with Barclays. I called and checked myself after you called last week.

The Barclays representative I talked to said he came in and arranged the transfer in person. There's no chance of error, I'm afraid."

The words were kind, and Niall pursed his lips, wondering exactly what Ian had told her about the situation. Niall doubted she'd disclosed the information about who made the payment to Ian—if she had, he wouldn't have needed to come out here—but no confidentiality laws would have stopped Ian from telling her about Ethan and Niall's suspicion Ethan had paid off the loan. Ian had been the one to float the idea while they'd been drowning their sorrows in too-strong coffee after their ill-fated outing on Romeo's Rowboat. He'd bullied Niall into telling him the whole story and offered surprisingly sensitive and helpful advice and insights.

Niall's entire body was tense as he gripped the sheet of paper. He wasn't sure what he was feeling now he had confirmation Ethan had been the one to pay off the loan. He wasn't sure if he should be angry with Ethan for doing something so huge without saying a word about it to him or giddy at the thought Ethan cared for him enough to do something so idiotic. Niall wasn't a charity case, for Christ's sake. He didn't need saving. If anything, he just needed Ethan to pick up the goddamn phone and talk to him.

"I'm sure he had good intentions," Stacy said, her voice pitched low. Niall could hear the caution in her words, as if she was afraid of startling him or sending him into a rage.

"I wouldn't know," he said woodenly, carefully placing the paper back on top of the small file. He'd seen everything he needed to. Ethan had made the lump sum payment a little over a week after leaving the island. But how had he known which bank Niall had used for the loan? They hadn't talked about it, aside from Niall mentioning the charter business hadn't gone as well as he'd planned, necessitating the return to real estate. Had he left paperwork out on the desk? He tried to envision his house the day Ethan had been there. Had there been a loan statement out on the table Ethan had cleared off to work on?

"Mr. Ahern?"

The concern in Stacy's voice was palpable. Niall forced a smile in response.

"I think I'll take that drink now, Ms. LeBlanc, if the offer still stands. Tea, if it's not too much trouble. And please, call me Niall. We'll be getting to know each other much better, I'm sure, while you arrange another loan for me."

"ROGER, I swear to God, if you don't stop I'm going to take that bowl and throw it out the window!"

Roger paused, spoon halfway to his mouth, and stared at his wife. Drops of milk splashed into the bowl, the sound noticeable in the otherwise silent kitchen.

"Stephanie—" Niall began, eyes crinkling with concern.

"No. I've had it with both of you." Stephanie cradled her forehead in her hands, the sleeves of her ratty bathrobe pooling around her elbows, which were propped on the table. "I need quiet. I can't think with all this noise."

Niall's jaw fell open. He and Roger had been sitting at the kitchen table, reading the newspaper and eating breakfast. He hadn't spoken a word to Roger since he'd come down, poured himself a cup coffee, and asked Roger if he'd wanted a refill. That had been several minutes before Stephanie had emerged from the bedroom and taken a seat at the table.

"You, with the chewing," she said, looking up to glare at Roger, who surprised Niall by looking chagrined instead of puzzled at the odd outburst. "And you," she said, rounding her attentions on Niall, "with your moping. Do you think I can't hear what's going on in your head? Jesus, Niall, you're the loudest thinker I know. Every thought is written on your face."

Stephanie stood, managing to look strangely menacing in her pink bathrobe. Niall wondered if perhaps she was in the middle of some sort of mental breakdown. Or maybe he was. Maybe this crazy-eyed, unkempt Stephanie was a hallucination of some sort.

He'd never seen her so frazzled, and that thought must have been clear on his face as well, since she rounded on him with a glare.

"It is not me, Nil. It is you, with your commitment phobia and your stupid, unfounded fears that you'll lose us if you move on."

Niall flinched at the use of his childhood nickname. It had died with Nolan; Niall couldn't stand for anyone to call him Nil anymore, and he knew Stephanie must be beyond frustrated to have used it. She hadn't called him that since the day after they'd buried Nolan, when he'd thrown a glass pitcher against the wall in her kitchen and forbade her to use it anymore.

Stephanie closed her eyes, her brain finally registering her slip. Her eyes softened in apology, but the tight line of her mouth didn't ease.

"Niall," she enunciated purposefully, drawing the word out. "He was my brother, and I love him. I miss him every day. But you're an idiot if you think I would ever turn my back on you for any reason."

Niall gaped at her, unsure of what to say. He watched out of the corner of his eye as Roger slowly lowered his spoon into the bowl, careful not to clink the metal against the porcelain. He didn't look overly concerned at Stephanie's outburst, which made Niall wonder if she'd yelled at Roger about his chewing, which hadn't seemed rude or loud to Niall, before. Would he and Nolan, he wondered, have had fights like that if Nolan was still alive and they'd gotten married, as they'd always planned to? He could almost envision it, the two of them seated at the small table Niall had wedged into the tiny breakfast nook at the townhouse, the one that could only seat two but that they kept anyway because it was all that would fit in the small, windowed nook. He should have put a bench there instead of the chairs, he noted absently, almost clinical in his inspection of the scene playing in his mind. Nolan's knees were hitting the edge of the table leg, and Niall wondered if they always had. Why hadn't Nolan ever complained? What else hadn't Niall noticed?

He blinked, pulled back out of his musings by Stephanie's sharp words as she berated him for not listening, something he apparently did often.

"You are Camille's uncle. You're my brother-in-law in every way that matters. I love you and I want you to be happy. You could fall in love a hundred times with a hundred different men and it wouldn't change the fact that for better or worse, you are part of this family."

Niall felt his eyes prick with tears, but he swallowed them back, standing stiffly and shuffling across the worn linoleum floor into Stephanie's open arms. He pressed a kiss against the side of her head and buried his face against her neck, the soft, fluffy fabric of her ridiculous robe tickling his nose.

"I don't approve of the way you're handling this business with Ethan, but I'm not going to meddle." Niall laughed at her obvious lie. "Much, anyway."

Behind them, he could hear Roger pick up his spoon and start to eat again, smoothing the wrinkles out of the sports section, which he'd laid down when Stephanie had yelled at him.

"I'll try to think quieter," Niall whispered, the words muffled in the voluminous fabric. He held her for another second, brow furrowing when he realized he actually could hear Roger chewing. After only a few seconds, the sound began to grate on his nerves and he suddenly felt awash in sympathy for Stephanie. "And as for Roger, I'll cook soup for lunch, shall I?"

Stephanie laughed, swatting him on the shoulder as he released her. She stuck her tongue out at Roger as she passed, her gigantic bunny slippers squeaking as she padded out of the room. When she reached the doorway, she arched a brow at the two of them.

"Roger will pick up lunch on the way home from the airport. Your plane leaves at two, Niall. Camille packed a bag for you. She said she's tired of you 'mooning around.' She also took the liberty of loading up your iPod for the flight. Be prepared for a lot of Justin Bieber. Apparently he understands heartbreak like no one else." Stephanie put her arm over her face, pretending to swoon. "And

Roger? I have a craving for Chinese. Maybe the place on Jersey Street? Chan's?"

Niall gaped after her as she gave him one final, stern look and flounced down the hallway, yelling something about being late to Camille, who merely turned up the music blaring from her room—good God, was that Justin Bieber? Niall wondered—in response. Business as usual in the Kendall household, aside from the fact that Niall was apparently being booted out.

"He's a tosser, but you haven't been this animated about anyone since Nolan." Roger usually didn't speak, especially not about things like relationships, so the words were doubly shocking. "She's been worried about you, holed up on that island like you're punishing yourself. Stephanie's right, you know. Nolan never wanted you to mourn him like this."

Niall blinked, looking up to meet Roger's eye.

"He used to talk to me about the possibility of him dying and how he wanted you to move on, back while he was still in the Royal Marines," Roger continued, unaware his words were making Niall's chest tighten to the point of pain. Nolan had talked with Roger about dying? About what Niall should do if he didn't come home? It was news to Niall. Nolan had never been anything but dismissive of Niall's own fears that Nolan might die in Afghanistan. It was dizzying to hear Nolan had been worried, and even more so that he'd talked to his brother-in-law about taking care of Niall if he did.

"He said you were too passionate and alive to be alone. He never wanted that for you. He'd hate that you're so isolated, Niall. And don't tell me you love the island, we both know you bloody well despise it."

Niall swallowed, the retort Roger had so easily shot down dying on his lips.

"Go to Seattle. See Ethan. And if it doesn't work out, come back here and move in with us. Sell the boat, sell the house. Jesus, sell that agency you hate so much. Just be happy, Niall. That's all any of us want for you, Nolan included."

Deep moment apparently over, Roger gave Niall a sharp nod and then picked the newspaper back up, burying himself behind it. Niall was absurdly grateful for the gesture, which was so British it made him ache for home as he blinked back tears. No one hid their feelings in Tortola. Everywhere—at the grocery store, during dinner at restaurants, even in the middle of the street—people aired their grievances like it was nothing. Roger's abrupt dismissal would be labeled rude and heartless on the island, but it was just the opposite. It was kind, giving Niall the opportunity to gain control over his emotions.

"Can't sell the boat," Niall said once the tightness in his chest had eased. He quirked his lips into a tiny smile. "Not with the shiny new mortgage I just took out on it."

"Well, then sell the damned real estate agency. The woman who works for you, Kesha, she'd buy it. She told me as much last time we were down to see you." Roger tipped the top of the newspaper down, looking at Niall meaningfully.

"Keandra, and yes, I know she will. She should have the deposit on the office building by next month. After that I'm going to let her pay me a percentage of the revenue until she's caught up."

"Are you sure it's not Kesha?" Roger furrowed his brow.

"You've been letting Camille pick the radio station too often, I think. Tell me, what grand words of advice does Justin Bieber have about love? Apparently Cammie thinks he'll help me sort out Ethan."

Roger laughed, shaking his head. "You'd best get a move on if we're to make it to the airport on time."

Niall looked back to the empty doorway, considering everything Stephanie and Roger had said to him. Steph was right. He needed to go confront Ethan, even if it was just to give him the check. But how did a guy return the money an almost-lover had gone behind his back to give him? Niall snickered as he wondered if Justin Bieber had ever sung a song about that.

ELEVEN

DESPITE THE harried start, Roger managed to get Niall to the airport an hour before his flight. It had barely been enough time to navigate his way through security, which he'd done while alternately cursing Stephanie for booking the ticket and mentally praising Camille for packing him a bag small enough it didn't need to be checked. It wasn't until he'd gotten on the plane that he'd realized she hadn't really put anything useful in the bag, aside from his iPod, a few pairs of boxers and what looked like a two-year supply of gummy worms. Luckily, Niall had managed to change his return flight when he'd checked in. He had no intention of spending any more time in Seattle than he had to, although it meant a long day of traveling. It was even worth the funny look from the booking agent for switching to a same-day return flight.

By the time Niall had collapsed into the too-small airplane seat, sandwiched between an old man and a woman in her early twenties, he was sweaty and tense with the beginnings of a headache curling up his neck.

"Would you like one?"

Niall looked up, fighting the urge to shake his head to clear the fog in his brain. He'd been staring out the window through the half-opened shade, but apparently the woman thought he'd been looking at her.

"I'm sorry?"

"You were looking at my protein bar," she said, gesturing with the beige-colored bar in her hand, which until that moment Niall hadn't realized was food. It certainly didn't look like food. "I have several, if you'd like one. I always bring extra on long flights."

Niall studied her, eyes narrowed a bit. She was a slip of a thing, probably because she never ate any real food. He had a fleeting urge to feed her.

"That's kind of you, but I'm fine." He rifled through his bag, hoping to end the conversation by finding something to read so he looked occupied, but Camille hadn't thought to pack any books or magazines. He supposed it would be even ruder to listen to his iPod, but he really wasn't in the mood to talk.

"Are you sure? You look a little peaked. Have you eaten today?" The woman twisted in her seat so she could get a better look at him, her lips pursed as she took inventory of his flushed cheeks and tense shoulders. "We could probably get a glass of water or some juice for you from the flight attendant. You look dehydrated."

Niall stared at her, not sure how to respond. She didn't seem to notice his silence, barreling on with a diatribe about the importance of drinking enough water while on a flight and the general poor health practices that consumed today's society.

"Airline regulations today make it so difficult for travelers to take proper care of themselves," the woman was saying, her expression animated as she berated airport security for not allowing passengers to bring bottles of water with them through the checkpoints.

"I always bring an empty bottle with me to fill up at a water fountain once I've reached my terminal," she said, rummaging through her bag and coming up with a garishly pink aluminum bottle that was scraped and dented from heavy use. "I take it with me everywhere. Clips right on to my belt when I'm rock climbing, even, see?"

She pointed to the small carabiner clip, and Niall felt himself nod, completely caught off guard by the woman and her seeming ability to talk without stopping for breath. Rock climbing explained the dents in the bottle, at least.

"What am I doing? Oh, Clary Sage Smith, what is your problem? You'd think you'd never met a good-looking man, before," she muttered to herself. Niall wondered if she'd intended for him to hear her quiet aside or not.

"I apologize. I get a little carried away sometimes," she said, thrusting her hand into the space between them. He took it automatically, as surprised by her firm grip as he had been by her enthusiastic speech about hydration. "Clare Smith. Self-avowed hydration nut and soon-to-be naturopath, in case you hadn't guessed."

Not only hadn't Niall guessed, he didn't even know what that was. He said as much after he introduced himself and reclaimed his hand, which Clare had begun examining.

"You have lovely skin, but I can see some sun damage there and some definite puckering from dehydration. You really should have something to drink. Noncaffeinated, of course. The worst thing you can do on an airplane is drink a diuretic."

She offered him the pink bottle again and Niall shook his head. He wondered if everyone who met Clary Sage Smith felt this overwhelmed, or if it was the confined space and lack of sleep that had Niall's head spinning. He'd noticed she'd introduced herself as Clare instead of Clary Sage, which was the name she'd used while chastising herself. It made him wonder if her eccentricities had been inherited along with her strange name. She'd probably grown up on a commune, he mused.

"I'm studying to be a doctor," she said, pushing the button on their joined seats that called the flight attendant. When the harried woman made her way through the tiny aisle to them, Clare asked her for a bottle of water, telling the flight attendant Niall wasn't feeling well.

"A doctor?" Niall raised a brow.

"Well, a doctor of alternative medicine. That's what naturopathy is. But I know dehydration when I see it." She took the cup from the tight-lipped flight attendant, who clearly wasn't happy with being asked to fetch a drink before beverage service had begun.

"Thank you," Niall said, touching the flight attendant's elbow lightly. She offered him a small smile, charmed by his accent. He found that most American women—and some men—were, and Niall ruthlessly used it to his advantage.

"The drink cart will be along in a few minutes if you'd like something other than water," she said, blushing slightly when Niall smiled.

"Niall? Your drink?" Clare nudge Niall's hand with the water, holding a napkin out in her other hand.

"Clare, I appreciate your concern, but—" Niall trailed off when she dived back into her enormous purse, this time pulling out several bottles of pills.

"This is St. John's wort." She placed two beige capsules in his hand alongside the water. "Drink up, it's never a good idea to swallow pills dry."

Niall gaped, looking from his hand to Clare. She was a complete stranger and she expected him to take some random medication from her?

"It's obvious you aren't sleeping well. I can tell from the circles under your eyes and the way your skin is a bit pale even underneath your tan." She fixed him with a stern look that would have done Stephanie proud. "You should be wearing sunscreen, you know. Any tan at all is evidence of sun damage. And I doubt you take supplements or eat enough antioxidant-heavy food to deal with all those free radicals."

"Really, I'm—"

"I can tell you have a lot on your mind. You're dressed casually, so I'd say you're headed to Seattle for personal reasons, not professional. You are heading to Seattle, right? It's not a layover to somewhere else?"

Niall nodded despite himself, too captivated by Clare and her complete and utter lack of propriety to notice he was only encouraging the madness.

"Right. So you're going to Seattle to see someone. You aren't happy about it, I can tell from the tight lines around your eyes and mouth. That, coupled with your apparent lack of sleep, probably means you're quarreling with someone close to you. A lover, I'd say, because if it was a family member I doubt you'd be so nervous."

Niall opened his mouth to tell her he wasn't nervous, but Clare's gaze drifted down to the armrest, where he was drumming his fingers tunelessly. He clenched them into a fist, moving his arm off the armrest and placing it in his lap.

"St. John's wort is an herbal supplement people have taken for centuries to help ward off the effects of depression, sleep deprivation and headaches," she said, arching an eyebrow when Niall would have protested that he wasn't depressed. "I'm certain you suffer from the last two and probably even a touch of the first, as well."

"It's really none of your business." Niall was a bit surprised at himself for snapping at a stranger, but Clare seemed to be pushing all the right buttons. Once he'd managed to shrug off his shock at her audacity, he found himself getting angry.

Clare shrugged, picking a magazine about acupuncture up out of her lap and opening it to the page she'd been reading.

"Suit yourself." She kicked his bag open with the toe of her shoe and dropped the bottle of St. John's wort into it. The pills rattled inside as the bottle rolled to the bottom of his bag. "Two a day until your sleep schedule—or your love life—sorts itself out."

Niall gave her a measured look, ignoring the bottle in favor of putting his earphones on and fiddling with his iPod. He no longer cared if it looked rude; he just wanted to be done with the conversation.

What blared in his ears sounded more like something from a high school talent show than anything Niall would call music, and he wrinkled his nose at the unfamiliar song, wondering if he'd taken Camille's iPod by mistake. Then he remembered Stephanie's warning that his niece had loaded her favorite love songs onto his to help him get in the right frame of mind for his confrontation with Ethan.

He thumbed at the dial, squinting at the screen when it brightened. Well, that explained it. Apparently he'd just had his introduction to Justin Bieber. The boy kept crooning about hearts under attack and Niall ripped the earphone jack out of the iPod in disgust. There was no way he was going to suffer through the prepubescent idiocy Camille had apparently thought would help him. Niall figured his first foray into the preteen singing sensation had been a twofer, as his cousin Royce liked to say—first and last.

Suddenly not so keen on listening to music, Niall leaned forward and grabbed the only reading material available, aside from the information card. He flicked through the worn and dog-eared copy of the Sky Mall, perking up when he found the robotic panda bear that would whimper and cry if not given attention. And it sang. Perfect. Camille's birthday was coming up, and he owed Stephanie a little payback.

AFTER SPENDING a brutal two hours watching the in-flight movie, Niall gave in to the inevitable and turned to Clare, who'd been gracious about not complaining when he elbowed her every time he moved. The man on his other side easily took up all of his own seat and nearly a third of Niall's as well, and as a result Niall had been practically sitting in Clare's lap for most of the flight.

"So, how far along are you in your homeopathy studies?" he asked when she looked up from her book.

"It's naturopathy, actually. It's a common mistake," she said, putting her book aside and greeting Niall with a sunny smile. "They deal in many of the same elements, but naturopathy is more grounded in science."

Niall's brow rose as he contemplated that, and Clare rushed on, cheeks pinking.

"Not that I'm discrediting homeopathy. I'm not. There are many skilled practitioners out there," she said, stumbling over her words as her blush deepened. "I hate it when people put down naturopathy, and here I am doing it to another branch of alternative medicine."

"No homeopaths to offend here. Your momentary slip can be our secret," Niall said, grinning. She'd come on strong at first, but he had to admit Clare was growing on him. Her eagerness was almost painful to witness, but he couldn't deny she was genuinely warm and unabashedly friendly.

"Anyway, I'm in my last semester. I was actually back home in Newark for a job interview this weekend, but I think I might miss the Pacific Northwest too much if I left."

"Sounds like Newark isn't exactly home anymore," Niall said, understanding exactly how thrilling it could be to escape familiar surroundings and build a new life.

"I've spent the last eight years in school out there, and my brother and his partner live in Portland, so yeah, I guess it is."

"Eight years, eh? That's a seriously involved naturopathy program."

Clare snorted. "I have undergraduate degrees in biology and psychology from Gonzaga, which is in Spokane. I'm in Seattle now, at Bastyr."

"Hedging your bets on the woo-woo medicine, then, with respectable science degrees?" Niall couldn't help but tease her, she was just so earnest.

"You sound just like my brother Frank," she said, wrinkling her nose. "Like I said, naturopathy is rooted in science. My science degrees have served me really well in my studies."

Niall resisted the urge to tap a finger against the freckles on her nose. He felt oddly drawn to her, and it made him wonder if he was really so attention-starved from his virtual hermitage in Tortola that he'd latched on the first person who had a kind word for him.

"Frank? I'd figure your siblings would have names like Blossom and Storm. Frank doesn't go very well with Clary Sage, you know?"

She blushed. "You heard that, did you? Well, I'll have you know Frank is actually short for Frankincense. I have an older sister named Marjoram, who goes by Margie, and a younger sister named Rosemary, who is the only one of us who uses her legal name for anything other than paying her taxes."

"And talking to herself?"

"I don't normally talk to myself out loud, nor do I usually call myself Clary Sage when I do. But I just spent a week at home and my mother is a force of nature. She has ways of getting into your head. All mothers do. It's something they must learn during pregnancy."

Niall couldn't relate. He hadn't seen his mother since the last time she'd visited Tortola two years earlier. They spoke once a month by phone, but they'd never been close. As a kid, he'd spent most of his time either out sailing with his father or over at Nolan's house, absolutely in awe of Nolan's family. Their messy, noisy house was nothing like the quiet, austere atmosphere of his own. Niall couldn't imagine what his mother would make of a woman named Clary Sage who was studying alternative medicine. The thought made him smile.

"So Frank is out in Portland?"

Clare nodded, digging in her enormous bag for another protein bar. This time when she offered him one, Niall took it with good grace, his lip skimming back only a little as he studied the wrapper.

103

The package boasted about protein, fiber, and vitamins but was suspiciously lacking in any claims about taste. He tore it open as her urging and took a careful bite, cringing as he swallowed.

"It's an acquired taste," Clare said apologetically, offering him her pink water bottle.

TWELVE

NIALL WASN'T sure exactly how he'd allowed himself to be steamrolled into not taking a cab to Ethan's as he'd planned. At the moment, he was standing next to Clare at the baggage carousel, juggling a paper cup of awful vending machine coffee and nibbling on a Snickers bar that was very nearly good enough to justify the lecture he'd gotten from her when he'd bought it. She'd insisted on dropping him in the city since she was headed that way anyway and wouldn't give him a moment's peace on the plane until he'd agreed.

Clare was currently wrestling a large and garishly colored paisley suitcase from the conveyor belt. He wasn't surprised to see that as soon as its wheels touched the ground, she handed it over to someone else. The elderly lady gave her a pat on the arm as thanks and wheeled the monstrosity away, and Niall rocked back on his heels, taking another sip of now-tepid coffee. Clare had been at it for nearly twenty minutes, helping others with their baggage while waiting for her own to materialize. The paisley bag had been the last one on the belt, though, and Niall privately thought it wasn't looking good for Clare.

The carousel beeped ominously before coming to a stop, and Clare blew her hair out of her eyes and looked around the terminal, glaring at Niall when he grinned at her and toasted her with his coffee cup.

"I can still catch that cab if you need to file paperwork with the airline," he said when she approached him, tying her hair back in a messy ponytail with a band that had been around her wrist.

"No, it'll come. Besides, I told you I would take you to Ethan's, and I will," she said stubbornly. Even though he'd only known her a few hours, Niall knew better than to argue with her when her jaw was set.

Niall shrugged and took another bite of his Snickers bar. He wasn't sure how he'd allowed himself to fall so completely under Clare's spell, but by the end of the flight, he'd spilled the entire story about Ethan and his own international pursuit of the man who'd paid off his debt without even sending a note. He figured it was probably something to do with the fact that for all her Mother Earth mumbo jumbo, Clare was remarkably like Stephanie at her core. When she'd told him she was driving him to Ethan's, he hadn't bothered to argue. It hadn't occurred to him to protest—like with Stephanie earlier, he'd known it would be fruitless.

Clare had found his story wonderfully romantic, which made Niall wonder if he'd forgotten some integral part. Waiting for Clare to track down an airline employee, he reviewed his tale in his head. Supercilious magnate sweeps into town, is rude and demanding, flirts shamelessly and then leaves and never returns any phone calls. No, he'd definitely been thorough in his telling. Clare had taken Stephanie's view of Ethan paying off the boat's loan, which had annoyed Niall. It wasn't a grand romantic gesture. It was a payoff. Niall wasn't sure if it was because Ethan actually felt guilty about the way he'd treated him or because he was worried Niall might try to sell his story to the gossip magazines that liked to dog Ethan's every move, but either way it was unwelcome. Niall intended to make things right by returning the money.

Niall finished his meager dinner and tossed the remnants into a nearby trash can, fishing his phone out of his pocket so he could call Stephanie to let her know he'd landed safely. He told her all about Clare as he waited for the other woman to return, surprised when Steph actually found the comparison between them funny. He'd thought she'd tell him in no uncertain terms to grab a taxi, but Stephanie had actually thought it would be good for him to have someone with him who was on his side. Not that he had any intention of letting Clare stay past dropping him off, but neither woman had to know that. He didn't want an audience for the kind of things he was likely to say to Ethan.

Niall had just returned his phone to his pocket when the baggage carousel gave another loud beep, its lights flashing for a moment before it started to rotate again. A single suitcase came through the divider, most of its contents following in a box behind it. The suitcase itself looked like it had been ripped to shreds, bright-yellow caution tape holding its mangled sides together. Niall could see clothing and shoes peeking out of the rips, and as it came closer, he could see more of the same in the box behind it.

"See, I told you it would come," Clare said brightly, materializing beside him. She hurried over to the belt, grabbing the box while Niall took the battered suitcase.

"It's not the first time this has happened," she confided, and Niall had to smother a laugh at the total lack of exasperation in her tone. "I might have to break down and buy one made out of synthetic fabric. This one was manufactured with organic cotton and recycled bottles, but it doesn't look like it was quite up to the task."

Niall did laugh at that, but the airline official who'd followed her over was clearly not amused. Clare gave him a placid smile and took the paperwork the man offered her, signing her name with a flourish at the bottom before leading Niall out to the parking shuttle.

Niall spotted the cherry red Prius the moment he and Clare stepped off the parking lot tram. It didn't surprise him in the least when Clare made a beeline for it, gracefully skirting through two rows of cars as she closed the distance between them and the cheerful hatchback. He drew up short when she stopped several cars away from it, though, his jaw dropping when she unlocked a gunmetal-gray BMW coupe.

"That's your car?"

Clare grinned, opening the trunk so he could heft her suitcase into it. Her perfectly ridiculous suitcase she'd admitted she bought wholly on the strength of its reviews as a responsible, eco-conscious item, ignoring the fact that most people who'd purchased one said it wasn't suitable for heavy use. Like airline travel.

"Seriously, Clare. You lectured me for ten minutes after I bought a Snickers bar. You came out of the ladies' room with wet hands because it only had paper towels, not hand dryers. Most of your possessions came off the plane in a box because your green suitcase disintegrated. You drive a BMW? What about fuel economy? This thing must guzzle gas. What about the dangers of fossil fuels?"

Clare laughed, slipping into the car. Niall followed her, shaking his head at the leather interior.

"Hey, a girl's got to have some fun," she said with a shrug. "Besides, hybrids just don't have the oomph I need on the highway."

That was all the warning Niall got before she pulled out of the parking spot, her tires squealing on the pavement as she gunned it toward the exit. He'd hoped she was just making a point, but when she showed no signs of slowing down once they'd paid and headed out onto the main road, he started to worry. Buildings were flying by at an alarming rate, despite the fairly heavy traffic on the interstate. Niall closed his eyes when Clare nearly clipped the car in front of him as she changed lanes to pass it.

"Do you know where he lives?"

"I have his address, but I'm afraid I'm going to have a heart attack if I open my eyes to look for my phone," Niall muttered, shuffling through his pockets and coming up with his phone. He googled the address, letting the program read directions out loud so he didn't have to keep his eyes open.

A few minutes of blissful silence passed with only the radio and the automated voice giving them directions filling the car, but Niall knew it wouldn't last. He sighed when Clare broke down and started peppering him with questions about what he intended to do once he was standing in front of Ethan.

"I'm going to give him his check back, tell him it was appreciated but not necessary, and then I'm going to get in a cab and head back to the airport. I have a flight back to Newark in about four hours."

Niall was definitely regretting letting Clare strong-arm him into giving him a ride. His original plan had been to have the cab wait outside of Ethan's and get back in it to make the trip back to the airport; now he'd have to call one, which meant potentially standing around outside of Ethan's house for a while.

"You aren't going to let him explain himself?" Clare asked. Niall cracked an eye open, horrified to see she'd turned to face him, her attention focused on him instead of the road.

"Car. Car!" he yelled, squeezing his eyes shut again as Clare braked barely in time to avoid rear-ending the SUV in front of them. They were nearing the city proper, and traffic was slowing down, thank God, forcing Clare to slow along with it.

"Don't be so paranoid. I've never been in a serious accident," Clare sniffed, glancing over at Niall again.

Niall noticed she didn't say she'd never been in an accident at all, just that she'd never been in a serious one. It was not a comfort.

"And you didn't answer me. What would you lose by approaching Ethan and telling him how hurt you were by him leaving and cutting off contact? Worst case he really is the ass you've described, and you give him back his money and storm off. Best case he has an explanation, and you have the chance to salvage your relationship."

"We don't have a relationship," Niall barked, glaring at her incredulously. "Were you not listening when I told you what happened? We knew each other for a couple days and then he left. Ethan made it obvious he wasn't interested in pursuing any sort of relationship with me when he didn't return any of my calls. I don't have anything to say to him, and I don't want an explanation. I just want him to take his money so I can get back to the island and carry on as I always have."

Clare pursed her lips, and Niall looked away, focusing on the landscape around them instead of her frank stare. They were already into the city now, tall buildings blocking out the view and a steady stream of cars around them.

"I don't think you really mean that, Niall. He hurt you and you want to lash out and hurt him back, and that's OK. It's a normal reaction. But I don't want you to regret this a week or a month down the line. You have an opportunity to confront Ethan and find out what happened and I think you should take it."

Niall hated that she was right. As angry as he was at Ethan, he also wanted to know what had happened. Had he done or said something to chase Ethan away? Had it always been just a vacation dalliance to Ethan, and Niall had totally misread things? More than that, though, Niall wanted the opportunity to yell and speak his mind, letting Ethan know how angry he was. Niall hadn't had any closure when Nolan had died, and although this thing with Ethan was much less traumatic, Niall was damn well going to get some sort of resolution. He wasn't going to let this be something he dwelt on for years to come.

"I can't imagine he'll even see me in person," Niall said. "I'm probably just going to end up giving the check to the housekeeper or whoever else answers the door. I'd have mailed it if I could have, but I'm sure he'd just have ripped it up."

"And what's to stop him from ripping it up when you give it to him on his doorstep?"

Niall smiled thinly. "It's a cashier's check. Even if he rips it up, the money is gone from my account."

Clare clucked her tongue but didn't reply. Niall ignored the building silence for a while before breaking it. She really was exactly like Stephanie; he couldn't seem to best either one of them.

"If he wants to talk to me, and that's a big if, I'll listen, alright?"

She smiled. "That's all anyone can ask," she said serenely, turning down a street. She stopped the car at a looming iron gate guarding the neighborhood Ethan lived in.

Niall wanted to groan in frustration. He hadn't anticipated this, though he knew that was silly. Of course Ethan would live in a gated community. And by having the guard call up to the house and announce him, Niall was losing what little advantage he had. His daydreams about this moment had included Ethan looking absolutely shocked to see Niall on his doorstep; now he was probably going to be waiting for him at the end of his driveway.

"We're here to see Ethan Bettencourt," Niall said when Clare rolled down her window for the approaching security guard.

"Is Mr. Bettencourt expecting you?"

Niall shook his head. "No, but tell him it's Niall Ahern and that I have a check for him. He'll want to see me."

At least, Niall hoped Ethan would agree to see him. Though Niall had to admit, coming halfway across the world only to be thwarted by a gate was definitely something that would happen to him.

The guard disappeared back into the gatehouse, and Niall forced himself not to fidget. He was brimming with nervous energy, but he didn't want to show how strung out he was. Niall didn't want Ethan to know how badly Ethan had hurt him. He took a deep breath and resolved to keep his temper. He'd approach Ethan with cool detachment.

Assuming he could get in, that was.

The guard finally came back after a few minutes, tapping on the passenger's side window.

"Mr. Bettencourt said you can drive on through, Mr. Ahern. Will your guest be staying as well?"

Niall looked over at Clare, who seemed to be almost bursting with the desire to say yes. He wasn't going to have her wait around for him, though. Niall wasn't sure if the confrontation was going to take a minute or an hour, but either way, he didn't want an audience.

"No, she's just dropping me off. Actually, I'll need a cab. Can you call for one to pick me up in about twenty minutes?"

The guard looked surprised but nodded. "I'll call up to Mr. Bettencourt's when the taxi arrives, sir."

Niall nodded his thanks, blowing out a nervous breath as the gate opened and Clare started to slowly drive through. The homes lining the street were enormous, with intricately designed and pristine exteriors and landscaping. It was exactly the kind of place Niall could picture Ethan living, and also exactly the kind of place he himself could never fit in. No wonder Ethan had left him so abruptly—the differences between them were less apparent on Tortola, but here on Ethan's home turf, they were obviously miles apart.

"I don't want to leave you here by yourself," Clare said as she pulled to a stop in the circular drive in front of Ethan's home. As Niall had predicted, the front door opened as soon as she turned off the car. Ethan stepped out onto the porch, and Niall's throat clenched at the sight of him. Ethan was still in his work clothes, but he'd taken off his suit coat at some point and the sleeves of his oxford shirt were rolled up almost to his elbows. Though he was rumpled, it was the dressiest Niall had ever seen him, aside from the photos of Ethan from the Google image searches Niall had guiltily indulged in.

"I can stay," Clare said softly, putting a hand on Niall's forearm when it became clear he wasn't getting out of the car.

"No. I need to do this myself. But I can't thank you enough for bringing me out here and listening to me whine through the flight," Niall said, surprised to find part of his reluctance to get out of the car was the realization that once he did, he'd probably never see Clare again.

"That sounds suspiciously like a goodbye, Niall," she said, shaking her head. "You're going to call or e-mail me to let me know how your talk with Ethan went, and if you don't, I'll track you down myself."

They'd exchanged contact information on the plane, something else that Niall never did. But he did feel a bit comforted to know that no matter what happened, this wasn't going to be his last conversation with Clare.

"I will," he said, pressing a quick, impulsive kiss to her cheek. It had been the right thing to do, because Clare released his arm and beamed at him.

"Good luck!" she called as he opened the car door and stepped out onto the drive. "And remember, listen!"

Niall nodded, waiting until she started to pull away before he waved at her and squared his shoulders to head up to meet Ethan.

"Niall," Ethan said warily, watching him come up the walk.

As he got closer, Niall could see that despite the cool temperature, Ethan was barefoot. He was suddenly struck with the fear he'd interrupted something. What if Ethan had someone there? Niall wasn't sure he could handle seeing Ethan with another man.

"Ethan," Niall returned evenly, stopping a few feet away from him.

"You're pretty far from Tortola."

Niall clenched his jaw, holding back a bitter retort. "Yes. I have something of yours to return, but I haven't been able to get in touch with you."

Ethan stiffened, crossing his arms over his chest. The posture was extremely hostile, and Niall had to fight not to take a small step backward.

"I didn't leave anything of any importance on the island. If you'd called, you could have saved yourself the trip."

The words stung, as Niall was sure Ethan had meant for them to. At least he had confirmation that Ethan had never considered him important, no matter how much it hurt.

"You weren't returning my messages," Niall said, his tone clipped. "You couldn't do me the courtesy of calling me back, so I was forced to take more drastic measures to talk to you."

113

"I did call you. I called your office a few days after I left, and your assistant told me you were involved with someone else, so forgive me if I didn't want to return your messages just so you could tell me you'd already moved on. Jesus, Niall, I hadn't even been gone a week."

Niall blinked, his confusion bleeding into outrage.

"I wasn't there to take your call one time and what, that gave you the right to ignore the dozens of calls I made to you? I know you're a busy man, Ethan, but for God's sake, you could have just left a message. I'd have called you right back as soon as I was off the phone or not with a client. Jesus."

Ethan snorted, a murderous look on his face.

"I don't like to be taken for a fool, Niall. Don't be obtuse. I'm talking about you using me to cheat on your boyfriend."

"What the hell?" Niall suddenly wondered if the confusion he'd felt after he'd hit his head on the Orion had been a factor of being near Ethan, not a concussion. He was definitely hale and hearty this time, but his head was swimming all the same. "You're the one who left without a word! If anyone is the fool here, it's me."

Their voices were rising as the argument became more heated. Ethan lifted his head, looking down the street as he seemed to realize they were still on his porch. He opened the door, glaring at Niall until Niall took the hint and stepped inside. The foyer was huge, easily as big as Niall's small house, and Niall resisted the urge to look around. He wasn't there to get a tour of Ethan's house, he was there to make Ethan take his money back so Niall could get over him.

"Give it up, Niall," Ethan snapped after he'd closed the door behind them. "I know you're dating someone. I'd like to give you the benefit of the doubt and say I believe you weren't with this Chris guy when I was there, but I have to say your track record is a bit damning."

"Keandra said I was dating someone?" It wouldn't have been like her to divulge that information to a client even if he had been on a date, and Niall most certainly hadn't been. The week after Ethan left he'd been too miserable to do much more than go to work and slog through the day, counting down the hours until he could go home and lounge on the couch. Because of the damage from Thalia, he hadn't even had any showings that week, which meant he'd spent all of his time at the office. If Ethan had called, why hadn't Keandra put him through? She'd known he was waiting on a call from him.

Ethan made a sharp, impatient sound.

"She implied it. Though apparently it wasn't serious, because a few weeks later you were out with some other guy."

Niall felt like the floor had been kicked out from under his feet. What was Ethan talking about? Where was he getting this information about all of the supposed dates Niall had been on? Had he been checking up on him? Why sneak around like that instead of just returning Niall's calls? And what right did Ethan have acting like he was the injured party? Ethan was the one who'd left.

"Listen, I don't know what you're talking about—" Niall didn't get the full sentence out before Ethan rounded on him, eyes full of fire.

"I'm talking about the fact that I misjudged you so badly. I thought you were a nice guy. A great guy. I don't know who I'm angrier with, you for turning out to be the same brand of cheating asshole as everyone else I've dated or me for falling for your 'I don't do this, I'm not into casual sex' routine."

Niall still had no idea what had Ethan so upset, but he was livid at the implications Ethan was making. "You're the one who left without even saying good-bye!"

Niall pressed the heels of his palms against his eyes and took a deep breath. This wasn't how it was supposed to go. He'd spent a lot of time practicing his speech. He was going to be calm and professional. He was going to insist Ethan take his money back and then tell him if he was still interested in buying property on the islands—and Niall sincerely hoped he was—then he'd be more than happy to continue seeing him, on a professional basis, until they found the right home for him. Nowhere in his plan had he envisioned himself screaming at Ethan in his foyer. At least they weren't still out on the front step, Niall thought darkly. Even as secluded as Ethan's house was, he was certain their raised voices must have attracted unwanted attention.

Ethan hadn't responded to Niall's accusation at all, and Niall took another fortifying breath and pushed on. He could still accomplish part of his plan, at least. It looked doubtful that Ethan would want to continue doing business with him, which made what he was about to do even stupider, but the only thing Niall had left was his pride, and he'd be damned if Ethan took that away, too.

"Here." He shoved a thin envelope at Ethan, who took it automatically. Ethan's expression was still furious, his jaw set as though it was made of stone. Niall hesitated when he saw something flash through Ethan's eyes that looked a lot like hurt, but he chalked it up to a trick of light; after all, what did Ethan have to be hurt about? "It isn't for the full amount, because I couldn't get a loan for that much, even using the boat as the collateral. It's most of it, though, and I'll send you monthly payments until—"

Niall's words choked off when Ethan tore the envelope in half without looking at it, his gaze still locked on Niall's.

"Fuck, Ethan. Jesus, that was a cashier's check. Tearing it up doesn't make it go away. The money's yours."

Niall sighed, running a hand through his hair. "Look. Maybe you were guilty for leaving and thought paying off my boat would make up for it. Or maybe you get off on random acts of weird kindness. I don't know. But no matter what your reasoning, I can't let you do it. I'm sure $400,000 is just a drop in the bucket for you, but I don't want it. I don't want to be indebted to you. Isn't it enough that every time I'm on the Orion now I think about waking up next to you? I don't want to have to be grateful when all I really want to do is forget you were ever on the goddamn boat in the first place."

The color seemed to be draining from Ethan's face, and Niall didn't know if that was a good sign or not. He'd really thought he could keep his cool when confronting Ethan, but he should have known he wouldn't be able to. Two months later, the hurt was still fresh. It was made worse by the realization that Niall knew it was ridiculous to be so affected by a man he'd spent just two days with. He'd essentially guaranteed he'd lose Ethan as a client the moment he'd decided to fly out to Seattle to confront him, but it hadn't been something Niall had actually thought about until just now. It was worth it to him to lose such a huge commission if it meant he could salvage his pride, but even that was looking less and less likely the longer he stood in Ethan's foyer.

"You expect me to believe you were all torn up by me leaving? Right. You didn't waste any time letting the bed get cold, did you?" The fury in Ethan's words made the hair on the nape of Niall's neck prickle. He had to fight the urge to take a step back. "Did you let Chris buy you things? Dinner, maybe? Because I'd bet the percentage of his yearly income he spent taking you to dinner at Frenchman's Lookout was probably more than the percentage of mine I spent paying off your boat."

Niall could hear the drum of his heartbeat in his ears as his temper exploded at the provocative words. His hands were fisted at his sides, flexed tight to keep himself from grabbing Ethan by his lapels and shoving him into the wall.

"Who the hell is Chris? I have no fucking idea what you're talking about, Ethan!"

Ethan sneered. "And I suppose you don't know who Ian is, either?"

That brought Niall up short. How did Ethan know about Ian? And what the hell did Ian have to do with anything, anyway? Ethan took his confused silence as guilt, his sneer twisting into a grimace.

"What the hell does that have to do with anything, Ethan? I only came to return your money. I tried wiring it through your office, but your secretary wouldn't sign for it. She said anything of a personal nature had to be handled by you, and you weren't returning my phone calls."

"Yes, you've been really broken up about—how did you phrase it? Thinking about me every time you're on the Orion? Is that why you took that guy Ian's boat out instead of yours?"

"God, Ethan. What the fuck are you even talking about? Ian's just a friend."

"Do you always kiss your friends?" Ethan's lips were a grim, bloodless line, but his eyes were burning with an intensity that made Niall want to take a step back.

"Have you had someone spying on me?" Niall asked incredulously. The idea that Ethan had kept tabs on him but couldn't be bothered to pick up the phone and talk to him made Niall's head spin. Why was Ethan acting like he cared? Like he had a right to care? And what did Ian have to do with Ethan paying off the Orion?

Niall actually did take a step back when Ethan advanced on him, looking like a dangerous animal coiled to strike, his muscles sleek and tensed.

"So you don't deny it?"

It was becoming clear that nothing Niall could say would diffuse the situation, not that he was sure what the situation was. Niall had come prepared to give Ethan a list of reasons why he shouldn't have meddled in his financial affairs, not to talk about supposed dalliances he'd had with other men.

"Of course I deny it! Not that it's any of your business, but Ian is a friend. An overly amorous friend who tries to kiss pretty much anything that moves, and when he tried it on me, I let him know in no uncertain terms that if he did it again he'd regret it. Did your source not tell you that part?"

Niall's chest heaved, his pulse racing from outrage. Ethan had no right to be checking up on him. If he wanted to sleep with Ian, he was free to do so. Hell, if he wanted to sleep with half the island he could. He didn't owe any explanations to Ethan. What infuriated Niall even more was that he couldn't stop the words from spilling from his lips.

"I haven't had sex in over four years. I don't know who you think I've been seeing since you left, but you're wrong. You're the only man I've been interested enough in to want to invite into my bed and look at how that turned out. God. You think you feel like kicking yourself for misjudging me? I can't believe I actually thought we might be able to have a relationship. Fuck. I'm such an idiot."

Ethan looked slightly confused, but quickly mastered his expression, his face turning cold again.

"Fine. Even if Ian is just a friend, you can't say that about Chris."

"Chris. You keep talking about Chris. Who the fuck is Chris?"

"You tell me! When I called, your assistant said you'd been waiting for his phone call all week."

Niall narrowed his eyes, his pulse still racing. "What exactly did she say?"

"Does it matter?" Niall glared at him in response and Ethan huffed a sigh and continued. "Fine. When I called, I just said I was a friend trying to track you down. She said I should try you on your cell, because you weren't in the office, and when I said I'd left before I could get your cell number the week before, she squealed 'Chris, it's you!' and talked about how much you'd missed him and how glad she was he was calling. So I told her she was mistaken and hung up."

Niall didn't know whether to laugh or cry. Keandra hadn't said anything about the phone call, but if Ethan really hadn't identified himself, she might have thought she'd jumped to the wrong conclusion and hadn't told him because she hadn't wanted to hurt him.

"You're an absolute moron," Niall muttered, his lips twitching as he tried to contain his smile. Ethan in the grips of desperate jealousy was actually rather adorable, now that Niall understood what had happened.

"Excuse me?"

"She didn't mistake you for a man named Chris." Niall did give in and laugh now. He could see Ethan's jaw clench harder as he thought Niall was laughing at him. "It's island slang for 'good,' Ethan. Keandra was saying 'Good, I'm glad you called, because Niall has been going crazy since you left.'"

A crease formed between Ethan's eyes as he frowned and Niall rushed to continue, the words bubbling up out of his chest like water from a well, relieving the pressure inside. For the first time since Ethan left, he felt carefree and giddy.

"It's not C-H-R-I-S, like the name. It's K-R-I-S-S. It's not something you'd know if you hadn't been on the island for a while, and maybe as a tourist you'd never heard it, because islanders don't normally speak in anything but British English in front of—"

Ethan lunged forward, hands fisting in Niall's hair as he pulled him closer and cut him off with a kiss. It was nothing like the gentle kisses they'd exchanged after the hurricane had passed. It wasn't even like their first kiss, which had ranked fairly high on Niall's scale of passionate kisses. In seconds, Niall had responded by wrapping himself around Ethan's body, insinuating himself so close he fancied he could feel Ethan's heartbeat against his own chest. It was only his own, though, pounding so hard it nearly knocked the breath from him.

"Ethan—"

"Sorry," Ethan whispered against Niall's lips, peppering his face with dozens of tiny kisses. "My fault. I'm sorry."

Niall made a noncommittal sound, too caught up in their kisses to really register the apology.

"I came back, you know. I was so angry when I thought you were dating someone named Chris, but I decided maybe he was someone you'd been with before you met me. I left so quickly after the hurricane—and I'm sorry about that, I am. I got caught up in everything, and I panicked because it was way too soon for me to be falling for you, but I was. So I left, and I meant to call you as soon as I got home, but I didn't. And then the Chris thing happened."

Niall bumped his nose against Ethan's jaw, encouraging him to continue. His chest felt lighter than it had in weeks. He almost couldn't contain the laughter bubbling up inside him. He and Ethan really were idiots. At some point they'd have to work on communication, but Niall was too happy to dwell on that at the moment.

"You said you came back to Tortola?"

Ethan hummed, leaning his head back to give Niall better access to his neck. Niall kept nuzzling against the warm skin, rewarding Ethan for answering his questions.

"I did. I went by your house, but Mrs. Jim said you were out at the fancy marina. You were just docking when I drove up. The deck hands were more than happy to tell me all about your companion when I slipped them a tip."

Niall laughed. "I bet they were. I assume they also told you Ian's reputation as a rake who will sleep with any willing warm body?"

Ethan growled in response and Niall pressed a light kiss against his jaw.

"I didn't sleep with Ian. He's one of my closest friends on the island. Which isn't saying much, really. I haven't really been fit for human companionship over the last few years."

Ethan ducked his head and kissed Niall, slotting their thighs and hips together as he settled against Niall, pressing him into the wall. Niall sighed, relaxing against Ethan and enjoying the warmth of his body. His breath caught when he felt Ethan's tongue lick against his bottom lip, teasing him until Niall opened his mouth and let him inside to explore.

When Ethan's hands roamed from Niall's shoulders down his sides to cup his ass, Niall groaned and pressed forward, moving his hips away from the wall to give Ethan better access. The movement brought him flush up against Ethan's body and Niall's pulse jumped when he realized Ethan was every bit as aroused by their kisses as he was. He braced his feet and canted his hips forward tentatively, brushing their pelvises together. The friction against his growing erection made Niall grunt. Ethan seemed to take it as a sign, since he stepped forward, crowding even closer against Niall and pushing him back against the wall.

Niall wasn't sure if Ethan had misjudged or if he'd simply forgotten their surroundings, but instead of sending Niall back against the solid wall he'd been leaning against before, they'd sidestepped and were suddenly falling, crashing into the gigantic vase that sat near the corner, sending both them and a shower of glass onto the tile floor.

The fall didn't seem to bother Ethan, who resumed rutting against Niall's hip, his hand finding its way into Niall's trousers. Aside from being a bit breathless from Ethan's kisses and the fall, Niall didn't think he was injured himself, so he brought his own arms up, using one to caress the curve of Ethan's jaw while the other slid under his jeans and cupped his ass.

"Ethan!"

The shriek was enough to startle both Ethan and Niall out of their lust-induced fog. Ethan scrambled up, leaving Niall lying on the floor feeling extremely exposed despite being fully clothed. Niall bit back an obscenity, sitting up as best he could and trying not to blush like a teenager as Ethan started apologizing profusely to the older woman in an apron who had walked in on them. She was clearly horrified, if the way she kept her eyes averted was any indication, which helped ease some of Niall's own mortification.

"No, no. It's my fault. I am so, so sorry. This doesn't—I mean, you know this doesn't happen. God. Hortensia, I'm sorry. I apologize."

Ethan stammering and embarrassed was a new and enjoyable sight for Niall. Niall was able to see the humor in the situation once he got past his own embarrassment. He adjusted himself as surreptitiously as possible, awkwardly getting to his feet and brushing the dirt and glass shards off himself.

"Oh, God. The vase. Shit," Ethan said, looking at the mess on the floor in what seemed to be shock.

Had Ethan really not noticed it break, Niall wondered? Niall watched as the woman, Ethan's housekeeper, he assumed, opened the front closet and took out a broom and dustpan. Ethan held out his hand for it, his voice rising as she protested.

"No, no. I'll clean it up. It was my fault. It's late, anyway. Go ahead and go home."

They seemed to argue over it for a second, but finally the woman shook her head in exasperation and said something in Spanish that made Ethan blush and laugh.

"Hortensia, you are a gem. And I really am sorry." Ethan leaned over, giving her a peck on the cheek. He used her distraction to grab the broom and dustpan from her hands, provoking another string of Spanish.

"You don't mean that," Ethan said, quirking an eyebrow at her and shooting her a hundred-watt grin. "Go home. And I won't need you tomorrow, either. Not unless you want to walk in on another scene like that."

She blushed, shooting Niall a furtive glance before laughing and throwing her hands up in the air as she walked back out of the room.

"Should we clean that up?" Niall asked, nodding toward the broken vase and the dark potting soil that had exploded out of it.

"I'll do it. She'll be here for another hour or so, I imagine. There's no way she'll leave before she grills me for details. Why don't you go up and get settled into the guest room? You're staying, right?"

The words had a vulnerability that surprised Niall. Of course, everything that had happened so far that evening had surprised him. He certainly hadn't planned to stay at Ethan's house. He hadn't even planned to stay in the city. There was an eleven o'clock flight he'd assumed he'd be on headed back to Newark.

"Do you need me to send Joe to get your bag from your hotel?" Ethan asked, noticing for the first time that Niall had shown up empty-handed except for the satchel he'd taken the check out of.

"I don't have a bag. I wasn't planning to stay. I was going to go back tonight."

Ethan leaned against the broom, staring at him.

"You flew in from Tortola today and you were going to fly back tonight?" His tone was incredulous.

"Well, no. I've been in Newark. I was headed back there." Niall scratched at the back of his neck, frowning when he realized he had dirt and glass down the back of his shirt.

"I'll have Joe take you back tomorrow if you really want to go," Ethan said, a hint of something indefinable in his voice. "But you can't go back tonight. There are several guest rooms upstairs. Why don't you go pick one out? You can take a shower. I'll find some clothes that will work for you while Hortensia gets those cleaned. We'll go out, have dinner or something."

Niall wanted to protest, but the idea of getting a little time to wrap his head around everything going on with Ethan, not to mention a shower, was too tempting.

"Do you want help with that first?"

Some of the tension seemed to flow out of Ethan at Niall's offer. He shook his head, gripping the broom.

"I've got it. Guest rooms are upstairs and to the right. Any of them will do."

Niall watched him for a second longer, finally nodding. He turned away from Ethan slowly, as if he was waiting for him to say something else. When he heard the sound of glass scraping against the tile as Ethan began to sweep, Niall climbed the stairs, choosing the first open door. He wasn't sure what was happening with Ethan, but no matter what it was, it wouldn't hurt to be clean when he faced it.

THIRTEEN

THEY DIDN'T end up going out. Ethan's housekeeper had indeed stayed despite Ethan's pleas for her to leave, and by the time Niall had finished his shower and shrugged into the clothes Ethan had left out for him on the guest room bed, he could smell dinner sizzling on the stove.

Niall felt a bit ridiculous wearing Ethan's things, since Ethan was broader through the shoulders and a little taller, but he couldn't deny it felt good to be rid of the dirt and glass. Plus, the shower had given him time to cool off and catch his breath. He didn't want to stumble off the deep end with Ethan before they had a chance to sit down and really talk things through. He'd been caught up in the moment in Tortola, still giddy from riding out the hurricane and the sense of closeness being in a threatening situation with Ethan had engendered.

Now that they seemed to have a second chance, Niall wasn't going to let his hormones and adrenaline run away with him. Though he had to admit it was going to be hard to sit down for a serious talk knowing he was wearing Ethan's boxers.

He'd heard the doorbell ring as he'd been getting in the shower, and Niall had assumed it was the cab he'd had the front gate call for him. Niall felt bad about wasting the driver's time, but he was sure Ethan would handle it.

Niall took a deep breath, steeling himself for seeing Ethan again. He'd been upstairs for less than twenty minutes, but going down to find Ethan still required a little bit of mental preparation.

Niall wasn't sure where to find Ethan, which also made him uncomfortable. They weren't quite to the point where he'd feel at ease wandering around Ethan's place without him, which was strange, considering he'd had Ethan's tongue in his mouth only half an hour earlier. Instead, Niall followed the smell of browning meat to the kitchen, which by a happy coincidence was where Ethan was as well. The sight of Ethan's housekeeper lecturing him in rapid Spanish while brandishing a wooden spoon at him menacingly was enough to startle a laugh out of Niall, and the pair by the stove abruptly fell silent when they realized he was in the doorway.

"Don't let me interrupt."

Ethan flushed and the housekeeper arched a brow at Niall, pointing the spoon at him.

"You're the one who had Ethan acting like a lovesick puppy?" Niall's heart stuttered a bit at the accusation, color flooding his cheeks. When the silence stretched on, he made a strangled noise of agreement, feeling every bit as cowed by the housekeeper as Ethan had looked a moment ago.

"Good. Sit. I'm making dinner. There's a cake on the counter for dessert."

Niall grinned at the hopeful expression on Ethan's face. He'd never imagined the confrontation he'd spent weeks working up to would end with him sitting in Ethan's kitchen having dinner. It felt domestic in a way Niall hadn't felt in years; like being at Stephanie's but better. Niall couldn't explain why he felt so comfortable around Ethan; they hadn't spent more than a handful of days together, but their familiarity around each other felt like the product of a much longer acquaintance.

It wasn't all down to the two of them weathering the hurricane together. Crisis situations breed closeness, but Niall had felt like this

126

even before they'd spent the night being battered around on the Orion.

"Are you allergic to anything?" Ethan asked, snapping Niall's attention back to the kitchen. His expression was amused, and Niall wondered if he'd asked the question more than once.

"No. Whatever's cooking smells amazing."

"Everything Hortensia makes is great," Ethan said, earning himself a swat to the shoulder from the housekeeper. "She's still mad about the vase," he whispered conspiratorially.

Niall flushed at the reminder of what they'd been doing when Hortensia walked in on them. He definitely wouldn't mind exploring that more with Ethan later, in a decidedly more private setting. Niall took a breath, trying to remind himself that he and Ethan hadn't actually resolved much of anything yet. He hoped they could hold out for a real conversation before falling into bed together.

Hortensia whispered something to Ethan after she pecked him on the cheek, and Niall was struck by how close they seemed. He didn't know much about Ethan's family, but it was clear Hortensia was someone special to him. Niall stiffened in surprise when she pulled him into a quick hug as she was leaving the kitchen.

"I'm glad you came for him. He needs a challenge. You'll be good for each other," she said, squeezing him before letting go. "Dinner's ready. Leave the dishes in the sink, and I'll take care of them in the morning."

Niall was frozen to the spot in shock as he watched Hortensia leave. Something about Ethan seemed to inspire loyalty and true friendship from his employees—including enveloping Niall into the fold without question.

Ethan moved to get plates after she left, setting them on the marble breakfast bar instead of bringing them into the opulent dining room Niall had seen on his way down to find the kitchen. Niall was relieved that Ethan seemed content to keep things simple and eat in the large kitchen instead of making the meal more formal. The house was gorgeous and very obviously decorated with no thought to expense, but most of the rooms Niall had seen seemed impersonal. The kitchen radiated warmth and was the most lived-in room he'd seen since he arrived; Niall wondered how much time Ethan spent at home and whether he gravitated to the comfortable room with its homey feel. There was a plushly outfitted nook in the corner, under a window overlooking Elliot Bay, and Niall could picture Ethan curled up there with a book. He hoped that's what it was used for, and that it hadn't just been an afterthought from the interior decorator to fill the space.

"Hortensia was thrilled to make dinner. I don't usually eat at home, so she rarely gets to cook for me anymore," Ethan said as he dropped a trivet on the marble countertop and placed the still-steaming pan on top of it. "It's my favorite comfort food—red beans and rice. Nothing fancy, but it's delicious."

Niall hid his surprise that Ethan's favorite dish was something so pedestrian. Ethan had been comfortable at the casual restaurants on the island, but Niall had no doubt Ethan ate at Zagat-rated restaurants most of the time. Still, Niall doubted any dish Ethan had ever ordered at one of them could evoke the pure delight on Ethan's face as he took his first bite of the bean and rice dish.

"She makes the andouille sausage herself," Ethan offered between bites. "Isn't it amazing?"

Niall took a bite, unsure of what to expect. He was no stranger to rice dishes—they were a staple on Tortola, after all—but he'd never had anything that looked like this. It was slightly spicy, and he could definitely see why Ethan liked it so much.

"It's good."

"My grandmother was from Louisiana, and she always made this when she'd visit. I hadn't had it in years before Hortensia needled me into telling her my favorite foods from childhood."

"Do you have any family around here?" Niall asked, hoping he'd slipped the question in innocently enough that Ethan would think it was a natural extension of the conversation and not realize it was something he'd been thinking about recently.

Ethan's mouth tightened a bit, and he shook his head. "No. My father died a few years ago, and my mother has remarried and is living in Paris. I see her every other year or so. My brother's in Florida and I get down there a few times a year."

Niall swallowed the bite he'd been chewing, his hand shooting out to cover Ethan's without consciously thinking about whether or not the gesture would be appreciated. Before Niall could withdraw his hand, though, Ethan turned his own palm up and twined their fingers together.

"It's OK. I have plenty of people looking out for me," Ethan said, correctly reading the concern on Niall's face. "How about you? I doubt you have family in Tortola, but do you have any back home in England?"

"My father died when I was at university. My mother still lives in Hull, but I don't see her often." Niall debated whether or not to tell Ethan about Stephanie, deciding that if they were going to try to make things work, then he needed to be completely honest. "Actually, the person I'm closest to is my sister-in-law. She lives in Newark. I was staying with her before I came out here."

Ethan didn't look startled by the news, so Niall pushed on. "My partner and I never actually married, but we were together a long time before he died. We grew up together in Hull, so Stephanie and I have known each other forever. She moved to Newark with her husband, Roger, before I moved out to Tortola. I try to get over there to see them and my niece at least once a year."

Niall saw Ethan frown slightly, but the expression was replaced with a smile almost immediately. He didn't know if Ethan was reacting to the knowledge Niall had been in a long-term relationship that had ended when his partner had died, or if Ethan was upset Niall still kept in contact with his partner's family.

"So you have a niece? How old is she?"

"Seven, almost eight. Old enough to be cheeky but young enough to get away with it because she's still cute," Niall said dryly, remembering the Justin Bieber fiasco from the plane.

"Eight is a good age. I started mentoring Josh when he was eight. They definitely get sassier as they get older," Ethan said with a smile. He swallowed another bite, putting his fork down and shifting so he was looking at Niall head-on. "How long were you with your partner? If you don't mind telling me about him."

Niall put his own fork down, folding his hands in his lap. He didn't want to be touching Ethan while he told him about Nolan. Stephanie had succeeded in convincing Niall he wasn't being disloyal to Nolan's memory by pursuing his feelings for Ethan, but it was still hard.

"We were together for eight years, but we'd been best friends since we were small," Niall said, looking down at his lap. He knew part of the reason it was so hard to talk about Nolan now was because he never talked about him, but the knowledge didn't make it any easier. He did want Ethan to know about Nolan, though, and that helped. "Nolan was the stubbornest, kindest man I've ever met. He spent his life helping other people. He was killed doing it too. I was angry at him for a long time for stepping into a dangerous situation and getting himself killed—I still am. But that's how he lived his life, and I'm sure Nolan didn't regret giving his life to save someone else's."

Niall looked away, unwilling to meet Ethan's eyes. He didn't know what he'd do if he saw pity in them—he didn't want Ethan's sympathy. Ethan needed to know about Nolan because Nolan was a big part of Niall, but he didn't want Nolan's ghost to be hanging over their relationship.

Niall stiffened when he felt Ethan's warm hand close over his shoulder, giving it a gentle squeeze before falling away. When he looked over, Ethan was focused on clearing their plates and taking them to the sink. He started filling one side with water, apparently set on disregarding Hortensia's instructions to leave them for the morning. It fit with what Niall knew of Ethan, and he remembered Ethan admitting to being a neat freak while he'd done the dishes in the galley on the Orion. Niall also recognized Ethan's gesture for what it was—he was giving Niall time to compose himself. Niall appreciated it more than he could say.

Niall gathered the remaining dishes Ethan hadn't been able to carry on his first trip and stacked them, putting them down next to the sink. He leaned against the counter, watching Ethan methodically wash them.

"Nolan's been gone for a little more than four years," Niall offered after Ethan had put the last dish on the drying rack. "I moved out to Tortola after he died. Fresh start."

Ethan turned around, leaning against the sink. The effusive happiness that had been all over his face earlier was gone, and Niall wanted to get it back. He just wasn't sure how to move the conversation back to the present.

"Did it work?" Ethan asked, and his voice sounded a little rougher than usual. "Were you able to move on?"

Niall shrugged, stepping closer to Ethan. He held Ethan's gaze, slowly reaching a hand out until it touched the fabric of Ethan's trousers, his fingers slipping through the belt loop and pulling lightly. Ethan came forward without complaint until the two of them were pressed together in an embrace. Niall nestled his face against the curve of Ethan's neck, breathing in his scent and luxuriating in the warm skin.

"No, not for years. But then I met someone who made me want to try," he said softly, letting his lips move against Ethan's neck.

Ethan shivered in response and brought his hands up to curl around Niall, tightening their embrace. They stood in the kitchen like that for several minutes, content to be tucked together.

"We really need to talk," Ethan said, breaking the silence. The way he ran his hands up Niall's back to bury in his hair made it clear he'd rather be doing other things.

Niall leaned into the scalp massage, humming softly. They did need to talk. He wanted to tell Ethan more about Nolan and about why he had the Orion in the first place. And Niall wanted to know more about what had gone through Ethan's head when he'd decided it was a good idea to cut off all contact with Niall instead of asking him to explain what was going on when Ethan thought Niall was dating someone.

"It can wait." Niall knew he'd be kicking himself for saying that later, but Ethan's fingers felt wickedly good scraping against his scalp, and Niall wanted to give himself over to the sensation of being held by another person. It had been a long time, aside from the night they'd spent together on the Orion, which he hardly thought counted.

"I'll take you to breakfast, and we can talk then," Ethan agreed before he went in for a kiss.

"That sounds like such a line," Niall said, grinning against Ethan's lips. "I bet you use it on all the guys you bring back here."

Ethan pulled away, linking their fingers together. He led Niall back down the hallway and up the stairs and into the master suite. Niall was too giddy to pay much attention, but he got a general impression of clean lines and cool colors. The room was dark, the only light coming from a wall of windows overlooking the city and the bay beneath them. Lights twinkled on buildings and on the boats lit up in the marina.

"I don't actually bring many men back here," Ethan said. He ducked his head to mouth along Niall's collarbone, teeth scraping lightly and making Niall gasp. "I don't really do casual relationships, either."

Niall felt breathless from the kisses and the newness of the situation, but he was also a little shocked by Ethan's confession.

Ethan pressed against him fully before Niall could respond, the hard outline of Ethan's cock digging into Niall's hip as he ground against him. Niall felt himself harden completely in seconds, his own cock throbbing as he rubbed against Ethan with equal enthusiasm.

"Just… let me… please…." Ethan was fumbling with the buttons on Niall's borrowed jeans, fingers digging into the flesh of his belly as he struggled to unfasten them without breaking their string of almost violent kisses. He hummed in approval when he finally managed to get them undone, thrusting his hand inside Niall's boxers and wrapping his hand around Niall's aching cock with no preamble.

Niall groaned against Ethan's lips, torn between trying to thrust into the ring of his fingers and focusing on getting Ethan's clothes off. The need to see Ethan naked won out, and Niall broke the kiss so he could look down and open Ethan's trousers with trembling fingers.

"God, Niall. I need...." Ethan didn't finish. He caged Niall in his arms, holding him close as he pushed him backward onto the bed.

It gave Niall the courage he needed to slide forward, his denim-clad crotch brushing against Ethan's, making Ethan hiss in response and tug him down. Niall laughed breathlessly, nuzzling his lips against the stubble on Ethan's jaw. Ethan canted his hips up impatiently, and Niall smiled, his lips curving against Ethan's warm skin.

He kissed and nipped his way up over Ethan's strong jaw, pressing a soft kiss to the corner of his mouth. Ethan growled in response, turning his head so his lips were pressed flush with Niall's. Niall hummed in approval, slowly building up the kiss until he had Ethan squirming underneath him. He could feel Ethan's tongue tracing his lower lip, begging entry. Niall opened his mouth, groaning as Ethan's tongue swept inside and stroked against his own.

"I am going to undress you," Ethan whispered against Niall's skin, rucking up his sweater to kiss the soft skin of his abdomen, "and trace every inch of your body with my lips." Niall's breath hitched at the hoarse words, his pelvis bucking up, seeking contact with Ethan. "And then my tongue." Niall gasped as Ethan's tongue skirted around his bellybutton before dipping inside and nipping softly at the ridge of skin. "And then my teeth."

Niall almost whimpered when Ethan raised his head, leaving a trail of saliva cooling on Niall's stomach. He propped himself up, swallowing when he saw the look of absolute lust on Ethan's face. His normally blue eyes were several shades darker, reflecting the dim light in the room as well as the depth of his desire. Niall could see Ethan's tanned skin was flushed with arousal, his lips swollen from their kisses. The skin on Niall's own lips felt slightly chafed from Ethan's stubble, and he let his tongue flick out unconsciously, soothing over the sore skin. Ethan groaned, eyes fixated on Niall's lips, before tearing his gaze away and sitting up, caging Niall's thighs between his own as he fumbled with Niall's belt.

"But first, I'm going to finish what we started before we were interrupted earlier."

Before Niall could fully process what was happening, Ethan had climbed back up his body, claiming his lips in an almost brutal kiss. Niall didn't have the breath to protest the sudden switch, and seconds later he felt Ethan's calloused palm slip into his jeans and close around his aching cock, separated only by the thin fabric of his boxers. Understanding blossomed in his sluggish brain, and he groaned against Ethan's lips, eagerly rutting against his hand like he had earlier. Except this time they weren't in the hallway, they were in Ethan's bed, and Niall took advantage of having gravity on his side by fitting his palm over the curve of Ethan's ass, squeezing and kneading ineffectually until he realized Ethan had unfastened his own pants too. Since he didn't have to worry about staying upright this time, Niall bent his legs, using them to pull Ethan closer as he slid his hand down the back of Ethan's jeans, molding over firm flesh and making Ethan gasp and writhe against him.

"God, please." It took Niall a moment to recognize the needy, whiny voice as his own. He thrust up into Ethan's hand, fingers flexing in frustration.

Ethan reared back, and Niall tried to follow him for a moment until he realized what Ethan was doing. Niall settled back on the bed, watching as Ethan pushed his trousers down to his knees and exposed a hard, thick cock Niall hadn't had the chance to actually see earlier. His own dick pulsed at the sight, and Niall bucked his hips up, grabbing his boxers by the elastic and dragging them down as well. Niall's jaw tensed as his erection caught in the fabric, a whimper escaping his lips as he felt his arousal build from the sensation of the cotton caressing his shaft.

"Impatient," Ethan said, lips pursed in mock disapproval. He climbed forward, settling between Niall's thighs and aligning their cocks.

Niall gasped when Ethan's hand closed around his flesh, his cock caught between Ethan's hard shaft on one side and his callused palm on the other. Niall braced himself against the mattress, pushing his hips up and rutting against Ethan's cock.

It had been years since he'd been touched by anyone but himself, and Niall found himself spiraling toward climax at an embarrassingly fast pace. As excited as he was, though, it wasn't nearly enough friction, and the angle made it impossible to kiss Ethan. Niall let himself fall back against the pillows, then tugged gently on Ethan's cock until he took the hint, crawling up a bit so their cocks were flush again and Niall could wrap his hand around both of them, keeping them together. Then Ethan leaned forward and traced Niall's bottom lip with his tongue before delving inside, wrapping his fingers around their cocks as well, intertwining them with Niall's. Niall let Ethan set the pace, matching his strokes as he sucked on Ethan's tongue, his free arm curved around Ethan's back, holding him in place.

The feel of Ethan's warm skin above him was exhilarating. Nolan hadn't been Niall's first, not if he counted the two boys he'd fooled around with before realizing he was actually in love with his best friend, though they hadn't done anything more than frotting. Having another man naked against him was almost unbearably exciting, and Niall was glad for the sense of urgency. If they'd built up to this slowly, he knew he'd be full of anxiety. As it was, his world had narrowed to the feel of Ethan's cock against his and the press of Ethan's tongue in his mouth.

"God, Niall." Ethan rested his head on Niall's shoulder, panting as he rotated his hips, thrusting hard into Niall's hand. The desperation in his voice and the stuttering of his hips were enough to send Niall over the edge. His body bucked up as he came, his face pressed into Ethan's bicep. It felt amazing, like every nerve ending in his body was throbbing with pleasure, and Niall bit his tongue hard to keep himself from crying out as he convulsed.

Ethan groaned, thrusting into Niall's hand a few more times. Niall shivered when he felt Ethan's muscles tense the moment before Ethan's cock pulsed, his come joining Niall's in the cooling mess on Niall's stomach.

Niall continued to pump Ethan until Ethan pulled his hips back, causing Niall to release his softening cock. Ethan pressed another kiss to Niall's mouth, lips moving against Niall's as he rolled to the side.

When Ethan's cock slid out of his grasp, the weight of what they'd done settled over Niall. He could feel his already flushed, warm cheeks grow hotter as he realized his fist was coated with not just his own release, but Ethan's too. He was debating what to do—should he get up and wash his hand in the bathroom or just wipe it on the sheets?—when Ethan rolled over and grabbed several tissues from the bedside table, pressing two of them into Niall's hand as he used the other to clean himself up.

His blush still flaming, Niall wiped at his hand, then his cock and stomach. He'd avoided the awkward after-sex feeling by steering clear of sex altogether after Nolan's death, and it was hitting him full force. He didn't know anything about Ethan. Did Ethan like to cuddle after sex? Would he ask Niall to go back to the guest room? Ethan had said he didn't do casual relationships, so this hadn't been a one-time thing, had it? Niall could have kicked himself for rushing headlong into a sexual relationship with someone he barely knew, but the buzz from his orgasm was still too strong.

"I can practically hear you thinking from over here," Ethan said, laughing when Niall tensed guiltily.

Niall turned his head, holding his breath as he looked at Ethan. He didn't seem any different than he had been before they'd gotten off together. Laugh lines still crinkled his eyes, which sparkled with amusement at Niall's discomfort. Full lips swollen from their kisses, hair wild from Niall's hand running through it.

"Did you mean it?"

Niall blinked at the question, rolling up onto his side so he could face Ethan. There were several inches between them, and he was fully aware they weren't touching. He wasn't sure if it was a sign or not.

"What?"

"Earlier, when we were arguing in the foyer. You said you hadn't slept with anyone in four years." Ethan rolled up onto his side as well, reaching across the sheets to take Niall's hand in his own. He intertwined their fingers and Niall felt something inside him unclench.

"Yes," he said simply, not really wanting to discuss it further.

Ethan seemed to sense Niall's reticence and didn't press the subject, instead busying himself with pulling the sheet up and wrapping it around them. Niall scooted forward, burrowing against Ethan's chest. Ethan laughed, his chest rumbling against Niall's ear, and wrapped his arms around Niall, resting his chin on the top of Niall's head.

FOURTEEN

NIALL WOKE slowly, first registering he was in an unfamiliar bed and then realizing he was naked. Before he could panic, he felt the heavy arm around his waist, and he remembered he'd fallen asleep with Ethan tucked around him.

He was careful as he turned over, not wanting to pass up the chance to study Ethan while Ethan was unaware. The last time they'd shared a bed, Niall had been bleary-eyed from lack of sleep and his concussion, so he hadn't been able to truly appreciate how gorgeous Ethan was while asleep. Golden skin flushed from the warmth of the covers, jaw darkened by morning stubble, and hair tousled, Ethan looked nothing short of delicious. Niall snuggled closer. Ethan smelled musky and warm and undeniably male, and Niall gave in to temptation and pressed his lips softly against Ethan's neck, barely grazing the skin. It was enough to make Ethan groan softly and shift closer in his sleep, sending Niall's pulse skyrocketing.

Niall felt the awkwardness from last night rush back in, making him question what he was doing in Ethan's bed. Was he really ready for a relationship? Despite joking about it the night before, they actually hadn't resolved anything.

Ethan stirred before Niall could work himself up, kissing the side of Niall's neck sloppily.

"Don't tell me you're an early riser. We have to call things off before they even get started," Ethan said with a yawn.

Niall relaxed at Ethan's easy tone, back on familiar ground. "Not usually, but you did promise me breakfast."

"Note to self, Niall can be bribed with food," Ethan murmured, rolling so he was half on top of Niall. He nibbled his way down Niall's neck, stopping with a kiss below Niall's Adam's apple.

"Among other things."

Ethan grinned down at Niall. "Also good to know."

Niall shivered when Ethan ripped the blankets away, leaving them both naked and exposed. Ethan rolled out of bed and headed for the bathroom. Niall watched his naked ass, fascinated both by the ripple of muscle and the complete ease Ethan seemed to feel being naked. He envied him that.

"I have a conference call I can't reschedule this morning, so we have to get a move on if you still want breakfast. There's a little diner near my office. We could drive in together, and then you could take the car for the day to do some sightseeing."

Niall hadn't actually thought past breakfast, but it seemed like a good plan. He'd have to go back to Newark sooner rather than later, but he could spend a few days in Seattle with Ethan before he did. He'd called Stephanie before he'd gone down to dinner yesterday so she wouldn't be worried when he wasn't on the flight back to Newark last night.

"Sounds good. You can give me some tourist pointers over breakfast."

Niall climbed out of bed, wrapping himself in the top sheet. He shuffled over to the doorway where Ethan was standing, catching him with a kiss at the corner of his mouth.

"I'm going to shower in the guest room," Niall said, bending to pick up his borrowed clothes that were strewn all over the floor.

"Leave them. I like your clothes better on the floor than on you." Ethan's exaggerated leer made Niall laugh. "I'll bring something clean after your shower."

"I should pick up some clothes while I'm out today so I don't have to keep borrowing from you."

"I like you wearing my clothes," Ethan said, raising his eyebrows suggestively.

Niall dropped the clothes he'd gathered into a chair near the door and hiked his makeshift bed sheet toga up higher.

"On that note, I'm going back to the guest room to take a shower. When do we need to be ready so you won't be late for your call?"

"We'll be fine if we're out of here in the next forty-five minutes," Ethan said, waving him off. "Stop distracting me."

IT TOOK them closer to an hour, thanks to Ethan volunteering to help Niall dry off with a very thorough rubdown, but they'd finally gotten dressed and out the door.

Niall had been thrilled that the diner Ethan took him to actually had a full English fry-up and he was currently working his way through it, much to Ethan's disgust.

"Baked beans have no place on a breakfast plate," Ethan said for what was probably the third time since Niall's plate had been delivered.

Ethan had demolished his own omelet and toast like a man possessed, and Niall had blushed furiously when Ethan had implied sex always left him with a huge appetite in the morning.

"It's a very civilized breakfast," Niall said, taking a sip of his coffee. Most of the people he knew back in Hull would have balked at the thought of having coffee instead of tea with breakfast, but he'd always loved it.

"It's something you eat at picnics and barbecues, not with breakfast."

Niall was tempted to make a joke about this being their first fight, but he thought it was too soon after their actual first fight to do it. They'd talked a little bit more as they were eating about Ethan leaving the island and the misunderstandings that had come after, but it wasn't something Niall thought they'd be joking about anytime soon.

Ethan dug out his wallet and put a few bills down on top of the check. "I have to run, but you keep the car. I'll see if I can shift things around and take you to lunch, alright? I'll text you."

Niall rose in his seat to kiss Ethan goodbye, smiling slightly as he watched him hurry out the door and across the busy street. Ethan dressed in a suit was a sight to behold. Niall couldn't wait to get him out of it later.

He finished his breakfast, taking his time and reading the newspaper Ethan had handed him from the front stoop when they'd left his house. Niall didn't know much about Seattle, but Ethan had given him a few ideas about where to spend the morning. Pike Place and the Space Needle were popular tourist options, but Niall was in the mood for something a little more low-key. He was more interested in exploring the waterfront.

NIALL WAS sitting on a bench in the waterfront sculpture park when Clare bounced up, her smile almost blinding. He grinned in response, feeling like he was greeting an old friend instead of someone he'd just met the day before.

"I'm so glad you called!"

"I couldn't leave you hanging. You listened to me complain the entire way here and drove me to my doom. The least I could do was let you know how the story ended."

Clare swatted his leg as she sat down. "When you called to tell me you weren't heading back to Newark last night, I assumed it meant the story wasn't actually ending."

Niall suddenly felt a bit shy. "I don't think we're entirely sure what's going on, but no, it was definitely not an ending."

He'd checked in briefly with Clare after he had called Stephanie the night before, to let Clare know he was alright. She'd sounded so genuinely happy for him that he'd called again on impulse after he'd left the diner, inviting her to spend the morning with him.

"Well, it's great you two are working things out. You're a really good person, Niall. You deserve to be happy."

Niall looked down at his lap, smiling. "I'm beginning to think so."

Clare surprised him with a hug, squeezing him tightly before she let go. "Should we go do something? The aquarium isn't too far down, or we could head in and wander around the market."

"Isn't Seattle known for its coffee? Why don't we go somewhere we can have a cup and chat?"

Niall wasn't usually a very talkative person, especially when it came to expressing his emotions. Something about Clare made it easy to open up, though, and Niall found himself enjoying her company and her insights. She had a way of making even the complicated things in his life seem simple, and he definitely could use some of that as he tried to figure out what was developing with Ethan.

Clare shot him a sidelong glance. "Do I get more details about what happened with Ethan last night?"

Niall blushed, making Clare snort with laughter. "Not those details, but it's good to know you're getting some. I want details about why he left you on Tortola and how you two worked it out."

"Sure," he said amiably, standing and holding a hand out to pull her up off the bench. "Though to give you the short version, it was all his fault."

FIFTEEN

"HEY, BUDDY, something wrong?"

Niall put a restraining arm on Ethan's elbow, trying to stop him from intervening between what looked like a very private domestic dispute between a stocky man and a twentysomething-year-old girl with bright blonde hair and very obvious tear streaks down her cheeks.

"Ethan, this isn't our business," he said quietly, feeling uneasy. Niall had met Ethan for a quick lunch earlier and then hung around his office until Ethan had been able to get away for the evening. They'd had a nice meal at a nearby restaurant, and Niall was feeling pleasantly relaxed from the wine and conversation. It had been a lot like their first dinner together on Tortola, where they'd laughed and talked easily, simply enjoying getting to know each other.

They'd come upon the argument a few blocks from Ethan's car. The stocky man had stiffened when Ethan had spoken to him but ignored him, continuing to yell at the girl. She was curled around herself miserably, cheeks streaked with tears.

"Take a step back from the lady. It doesn't look like she wants to be talking to you," Ethan said, his tone more forceful this time.

The man harassing the woman started to turn around, and Niall's blood froze as he saw something metallic in his hand, glinting in the moonlight. The girl screamed and the sound tore through Niall as cleanly as a blade, filling him with fear and coldness that seemed to grasp his lungs like a fist. He watched, helpless, as time seemed to move in slow motion while Ethan, oblivious to the fact the man was apparently armed, took another step forward, hand on his shoulder to pull him fully away from the girl. It was shockingly like the mental replay of Nolan's death that had plagued Niall after he'd read the police reports, except ten times worse. Because this wasn't a nightmare, this wasn't an imagined echo of something that had already happened. Watching Nolan get stabbed in his dreams was horrible, but it was nothing like the prospect of watching the same thing happen to Ethan in reality. Niall's voice caught in his throat as he tried to call out to warn him, and then it was too late, because time sped up as the man turned from the crying girl, hand half-hidden under his coat, and rounded on an unsuspecting Ethan.

Niall didn't think; he just launched himself across the few feet separating them, caught the man from behind, and sent him sprawling to the side. The girl screamed again, louder this time, and Niall felt the pavement bite into his palm as he and the man hit the ground and skidded along the cold sidewalk.

"Take whatever you want, just take it! Tommy? Tommy?"

The girl's shrill voice cut through the fog of fear in Niall's brain, and he realized the man he still had his arms locked around wasn't fighting back. He could hear Ethan speaking to the girl, his voice low and calm. Niall risked a look up and saw Ethan had his hands out, showing her he was unarmed, as if he was the danger there, not the man Niall had tackled. Niall tightened his hold experimentally around the man's shoulder and was surprised when the man responded by whimpering slightly and curling into the fetal position. The silver object Niall had thought was a knife clattered against the pavement as it slid from his hand, and Niall saw it out of the corner of his eye—a cell phone.

"Fuck!" He let go of the man as if he were burned by his touch, scrambling backward across the sidewalk without even trying to get up. He'd tackled a man who'd been threatening Ethan with a phone?

"You can have my purse, my rings, just please, please don't hurt him. Tommy?"

Niall cringed at the girl's sobs, acutely aware he was the reason for them. They must have been having an argument when he and Ethan had walked past, and Niall had obviously overreacted to the man's aggressive posture when he'd turned on Ethan.

"—a misunderstanding. It looked like he was hurting you."

Niall could hear Ethan's continued explanation, the words careful and soft. His heart was still thundering in his chest, but Niall could feel color return to his face. He'd felt the dizzying sensation of the blood draining away when he'd thought the man was about to attack Ethan, but now Niall's cheeks were beginning to burn with the heat of his growing mortification. He wasn't sure what he should do. Standing might make the girl feel even more threatened, but he could hardly keep lying on the pavement. He needed to get up and explain, make sure the other man wasn't hurt.

The man who the still-shrieking girl had called Tommy sat up abruptly, cradling his left arm against his chest. Niall looked up, realizing Ethan had abandoned reasoning with the girl and had been crouched near Tommy, speaking softly with him. The man had a scrape along his cheek and there was a large hole in the elbow of his jacket, but he was able to get to his feet with minimal assistance from Ethan. Niall waited until Tommy was standing and speaking with the girl, who had gone quiet as she'd watched him get up, before standing himself. He kept himself pressed against the brick wall behind him, hoping to seem as small and nonthreatening as possible for someone who had just attacked a person out of the blue.

The police arrived as Ethan was trying to convince Tommy to go to the ER. Niall had been silent through it all, lips pressed into a grim, bloodless line as he watched Ethan try to explain and smooth things over. It brought Nolan's death back, making him question yet again whether Nolan would have been stabbed if he'd been there with him. Would he have been able to stop Nolan from intervening? Would it have gone a lot like tonight with Ethan, where he'd tried to stop him but hadn't been able to? Would the mugger not have stabbed Nolan if another man had been with him? Would two of them have been able to scare him off better than just one?

Niall had been certain from the moment the police arrived he'd be arrested and charged with assault because he harbored no illusions he didn't deserve exactly that fate, but Tommy had declined to press charges. Niall was sure it was all down to Ethan's diplomacy. It also hadn't hurt that Ethan had offered to pay all of Tommy's medical bills, in addition to paying for their honeymoon, which had been what the couple had been arguing about when he and Ethan had so grossly misjudged the situation.

As much as he disliked the humiliation that still stung his cheeks at his overreaction, Niall hated the warmth in the pit of his stomach at the way Ethan was handling things even more. The heat of Ethan's hand against the small of his back, radiating through his sweater, was almost as terrifying as the moment Niall had thought Tommy was about to attack Ethan. It was an absent gesture, meant to provide support and comfort as they sorted things out with the police, who had to take statements even if no charges were being pressed, but it felt like more. Ethan was marking Niall as his, protecting him, and Niall, despite himself, was letting him.

Niall hadn't realized he'd hurt himself until after Tommy had been taken back to be seen by the doctors in the ER, his fiancée at his side. Ethan and Niall had been left to wait in the hard plastic chairs in the lobby. Niall spent twenty minutes flexing his hand and trying to determine if he needed to have it looked at, but before he could concede to the pain and ask to see someone, the charge nurse appeared. He hadn't paid her much attention since Tommy had been taken back through the sliding door, so he didn't notice at first that she was standing there calling his name. When he didn't stand, she frowned and consulted her clipboard, calling out for him again.

Niall was puzzled, but Ethan simply stood and helped him up, his palm cupping the elbow of Niall's uninjured arm as he urged

146

him along. The superior smirk on Ethan's face made it clear he'd taken the liberty of registering Niall as well as Tommy when they'd arrived. The smirk only grew when the chief resident emerged, greeting Ethan by name and personally taking them back to a nicely furnished private room that was nothing like the tiny curtained cubicles they'd walked past on the way in.

Niall had always known Ethan was a wealthy man. They'd never have met if he hadn't been searching for a multimillion-dollar vacation home, after all, but he hadn't appreciated the actual scope of it until that moment. It made even more sense later, when he noticed the plaque with Ethan's name on it on the wall inside the nurse's station. Niall doubted it was a coincidence Ethan had brought them to a hospital he had apparently donated enough money to over the years to merit having the emergency department named after him.

There were so many differences between Ethan and Nolan, and Ethan's wealth was only one of them. Nolan had always been quiet and reserved around strangers; Ethan exuded confidence and authority, even with those he'd never met. The few times Nolan had accompanied Niall to the emergency room, he had been content to sit in the waiting room or melt into the background as the doctors asked questions and examined him. Ethan, on the other hand, was an active participant. He didn't hesitate to add details when Niall glossed over things or tried to downplay how bad the injury was.

It was annoying, but it also made Niall feel cared for, looked after. He'd always played that role in his relationship with Nolan; he'd been the adult, the one who remembered to pay the bills and ask the right questions. It was just one more reminder that Ethan wasn't Nolan. Niall could easily imagine being with Ethan as a partnership, something he'd never quite felt he and Nolan had managed.

The realization that he thought he was falling for Ethan had hit Niall like a bucket full of ice water. Niall had been certain he'd never find what he'd had with Nolan again, and he'd been right. As much as he'd loved Nolan, it had never felt like this. He honestly couldn't remember a time where Nolan hadn't been part of his life. They'd been friends for more than a decade before things between them had changed. There hadn't been any dancing around each other; they'd fallen into a relationship as easily as they'd fallen into their friendship. There hadn't been any of the butterflies or anxiousness Niall felt when he was around Ethan; with Nolan, it had felt natural and right. Niall liked that it was so different. It made it feel less like he was overwriting his memories of Nolan.

Niall wasn't sure what terrified him more: the thought he was being disloyal to Nolan and dishonoring their life together or the knowledge he was in completely over his head with Ethan and had no idea how to proceed. Niall suspected it was a bit of both. It left his head reeling in a way that had nothing to do with the painkillers the doctor had prescribed.

SIXTEEN

NIALL STUDIED the cast on his arm, experimentally flexing his fingers. The movement made his broken wrist ache, but it wasn't unmanageable. He wouldn't be able to drive for a few weeks, since the cast would make managing the gearshift in his Jeep impossible, but he didn't have his car here anyway, so it hardly mattered.

He'd woken up a few minutes earlier in the warm circle of Ethan's arms. They'd burrowed beneath the thick duvet, only Niall's broken wrist outside of their cocoon, propped up on several pillows Ethan had brought in from the guest room. Niall remembered sitting on the bed while Ethan rummaged through his drawers to find some pajamas for him, since Niall hadn't packed for an overnight stay and they hadn't bothered with pajamas the night before. Niall figured he must have fallen asleep, since he was still wearing his clothes. Ethan had taken off his shoes, though, and Niall wondered if Ethan had tried to wake him or if he'd just decided Niall needed his sleep and left him alone.

Niall was too warm under the covers in all his clothes, so he pushed the duvet back, shaking his head when he saw they were lying on top of the bedclothes that covered Ethan's bed. Niall assumed Ethan must have stripped the guest room bed of its duvet to cover them after Niall had fallen asleep on top of the covers. Ethan mumbled something unintelligible and pulled Niall closer as the

149

cool air brushed over them. Niall turned enough in his embrace to see that Ethan had forgone pajamas in favor of sleeping in nothing more than a pair of boxers.

Niall trailed the thumb of his uninjured hand over the line of Ethan's jaw lightly, not trying to wake him but unable to look and not touch. The stress from the night before showed on Ethan's face. Even asleep, Ethan didn't look completely relaxed. Niall was privately glad he knew that wasn't Ethan's default expression; he had the memories of the morning before to compare them to, and Niall knew when Ethan was perfectly content, his face was open and easy in slumber.

Niall felt a fresh wave of guilt over his behavior from the night before. He'd caused both Ethan and the couple a lot of upset, all because he'd overreacted. Ethan had been nothing but understanding, even before Niall had shakily told him Nolan had died in a mugging.

He curled back into Ethan's arms, deciding he was too tired to face the day yet. Niall smiled softly when Ethan responded subconsciously by pulling him closer. He let himself sink back to sleep, guided by Ethan's steady breaths in his ear.

WHEN NIALL woke again, the room was much brighter. The drapes were open, and he could see Ethan standing in front of the floor-to-ceiling windows, looking out over the bay. Like it had been yesterday, the sky was overcast, but he could make out a tiny bit of sun sparkling along the water in the distance. It was a gorgeous view, and it was easy for Niall to see why Ethan loved it so much. It reminded him of Hull far more than the views around Tortola ever had; the sight eased something hard in his heart. He was tired of the white sand beaches and brilliant blue skies on the island. Roger had been right about that much, at least.

"Awake?" Ethan hadn't turned, but apparently the rustling of the bedclothes had been enough to catch his attention.

Niall rose, padding across the room. Ethan hadn't gotten dressed, still wearing just a pair of boxers. Niall appreciated the view of his broad, tanned shoulders even more than the gorgeous scene outside.

He snuggled up behind Ethan, settling with his chest against Ethan's warm back and curving his arms around him, letting his broken wrist lean against Ethan's chest. He used his other hand to trace the outline of Ethan's nipple, teasing at the sparse hairs that surrounded it. "Trouble sleeping? I hear St. John's wort is good for that."

Ethan laughed. "It's past noon, lazy bones," he murmured, turning his head to nuzzle against Niall's jaw.

"You should have woken me."

Ethan bent around, capturing Niall's lips in an awkward kiss without dislodging Niall's hands. "You needed the sleep. We didn't get in until after 3:00 a.m., and those pills made you a bit loopy."

"Not too loopy." Niall pressed himself against Ethan's ass, his erection confined by the pants he was wearing.

"Mmmm," Ethan hummed, gently grabbing Niall's elbow so he could move him without tweaking his wrist. He turned, burying his face in Niall's neck and nipping at the curve of his shoulder. "I have a meeting at two."

Niall whined softly, arching his neck to give Ethan freer access to kiss a wet path across the skin. "Better hurry, then," he said, laughing when Ethan responded to his words with a scrape of teeth against Niall's Adam's apple and a low growl.

There was nothing rushed about the way Ethan undressed him, pressing openmouthed kisses over Niall's skin as it was revealed. Niall vaguely remembered Ethan threatening to explore every inch of him with his mouth the next time they made love, and he canted his hips forward impatiently at the memory. He didn't want slow and reverent, he wanted fast and hard. Ethan wouldn't be swayed, though, and he stilled Niall's hips by running his hands down his sides, fingers dipping below the waistband of Niall's pants and divesting him of them easily. By the time he'd helped Niall step out of the pants and underwear, Niall was squirming with the need to have Ethan's hands back on him. Ethan obliged, skimming with light touches over Niall's back until his fingers just touched the swell of his ass. Niall grunted when the hands stopped short of where he wanted them, Ethan's fingertips teasing over his skin with featherlight touches Niall was sure were designed to make him crazy.

Ethan's oral assault had moved past Niall's collarbone by then, his tongue sweeping out to cover Niall's right nipple with one broad stroke. Niall's knees threatened to give out when Ethan drew the nub into his mouth and grazed it with the sharp points of his teeth, but Ethan tightened his grip on Niall's hips, fingers digging into the soft skin of his ass as he kept him upright.

Niall walked backward as Ethan urged him to move, guiding him to a suede chair positioned so it had a prime view of the Sound. Niall sank into it gratefully, muscles tightening as Ethan followed him down, perching on his knees between Niall's open legs. He leaned forward, nuzzling against Niall's stomach and continuing to map out his body, lips and tongue following the slight curve of Niall's belly while his nose tickled Niall's bellybutton.

"Ethan, your meeting." Niall's protest was a weak one as he squirmed under Ethan's light, teasing touches. The clock on the side table showed it was nearly 1:00 p.m.

Ethan sat back on his heels, his eyes gleaming with amusement and arousal.

"Well, we'd better hurry then." His mock British accent was atrocious, but it made Niall laugh at the absurdity of it.

Ethan grinned, licking a broad stripe up Niall's naked thigh. Niall hissed out a breath as the warm, wet touch skirted his balls and continued up to his hipbone, where Ethan placed a loud, sucking kiss on the thin skin, the blood bruise already blossoming as he moved on, nestling his face against Niall's cock.

"Still want me to hurry?"

Niall fisted his good hand in Ethan's hair, tightening his grip in response to the teasing words. Ethan laughed again, his breath warm against Niall's thigh. He eased back, grabbing a box of condoms that had somehow escaped Niall's notice from the table next to the chair. Niall pressed his lips together, biting back a moan when Ethan shot him a predatory grin before opening one and rolling it down over Niall's shaft.

Ethan didn't waste any time before running his tongue up the thick vein that ran along the underside of Niall's erection, eliciting another hiss and a groan. Ethan used the flat of his tongue to bathe the shaft until he got to the head, swirling his tongue around it teasingly before obliging Niall's wordless begging and wrapping his lips around it.

Niall's fingers tightened in Ethan's hair, his other hand clenching into a loose fist despite the cast. He could feel his hips lifting up off the chair, seeking more of the warm wetness of Ethan's mouth, but he was too far gone to be embarrassed by his eagerness.

Ethan pursed his lips around Niall's shaft, sliding down it like hot velvet while using his tongue to shield his teeth and press firmly against the hardness in his mouth. He hollowed his cheeks, sucking lightly as he swallowed Niall down, not stopping his slow, torturous descent until his lips rested against the base.

Niall choked as he felt the sensitive head of his cock hit the back of Ethan's palate. Ethan swallowed around him, his mouth and throat tightening convulsively and then releasing him, and Niall let out a long, low groan to let Ethan know he was close. Ethan's responding chuckle sent vibrations up Niall's spine, making his limbs feel weak as all of his focus centered on the feel of Ethan's mouth around him and the tingling tension building in his belly.

He didn't know whether to be disappointed or relieved when he felt Ethan ease back off his shaft, lips and tongue swirling up until he had nearly released him completely. Niall stared down at the head bobbing in his lap, letting out a strangled cry when Ethan stopped tracing light patterns against the skin of Niall's inner thigh and began to tickle and tease at his balls, massaging them before moving them aside to stroke the sensitive skin of his perineum.

Niall's eyes widened as he realized Ethan was using his other hand to palm himself through his boxers, a darkening spot of precome visible near the waistband. Niall could see the outline of Ethan's cock every time a stroke pulled the fabric taut. When Ethan grinned wickedly around Niall's shaft, Niall realized Ethan knew exactly how much watching him tease himself was affecting Niall.

On the next upstroke, Ethan peeled his boxers down, letting them pool around his knees and exposing himself completely to Niall's hungry gaze. His cock twitched against the soft down below his bellybutton, smearing precome across the smattering of dark hairs. Niall's mouth watered, a jolt of pure arousal surging through him, but when he tried to sit up so he could return the favor, Ethan put a restraining hand to his chest and forced him back in the chair.

Niall locked gazes with him as Ethan bent back down very deliberately, curving his spine so Niall could see Ethan's free hand, the one not pressed against Niall's chest, had begun stroking lazily up and down his own shaft. The sight made Niall's neglected cock bob, excitement bursting through him before Ethan's mouth engulfed him again, burying him in warm, wet heat.

Niall struggled to keep his eyes open, not wanting to miss a minute of the show Ethan was putting on. He didn't think he'd ever seen anything as erotic as the sight of Ethan jacking off while sucking him. Ethan stilled once he'd swallowed Niall down to the base again, and Niall stopped breathing for a moment, waiting to see what he would do next. Ethan had closed his own eyes, hand flying over his cock in earnest. The vibrations from his moans sent cascades of pleasure through Niall, and Niall bumped his hips up once, twice, impatient for Ethan's mouth to move again.

Ethan merely hollowed his cheeks, and the suction felt good but wasn't nearly enough. Niall could have cried in frustration; he was hovering on the brink, but he needed more friction to send him over the edge. When he canted his hips up again, the head of his cock hitting the roof of Ethan's mouth, Ethan opened his eyes and groaned. There was no mistaking the lust in his eyes or the pleasure he'd taken in Niall's less-than-gentle treatment, so Niall did it again, his cock scraping along Ethan's lip-covered teeth as he fucked into his mouth, careful not to choke him. Ethan moaned again, moving his hand with sure strokes over his own shaft, curving his palm over the head of his cock as he teased at the precome there, letting it slick the way as he fucked his own fist.

Niall let go of Ethan's hair, using his hand for balance against the seat of the chair as he lifted his pelvis, his attention torn between watching his spit-slicked cock disappear between Ethan's lips and watching Ethan stroke himself in time with Niall's thrusts. Niall felt his control slipping, and he canted his hips up into the waiting heat several times in quick succession before he felt himself begin to crest, his muscles tensing as his orgasm burst from him, the searing pleasure making him forget to be careful as he worked himself into Ethan's mouth.

Far from being put off by Niall's roughness, Ethan responded by stroking himself faster, his moans joining Niall's a second later as he followed him over the edge, painting the delicate suede of the chair with his own release as he sucked Niall through his own climax.

Niall let go of the fabric, relaxing back into the chair as a languid laziness stole over him. He was flushed and panting, his arm aching from the way he'd been clenching his fingers. It couldn't dull the haze of satisfied pleasure that engulfed him, a pleasing mixture of exhaustion and exhilaration.

Ethan sat back, pulling the condom off of Niall's softening cock and tossing it in a conveniently placed trash can. He stood, stretched, and then bent over Niall. Up close Niall could see how red and swollen Ethan's mouth was, and the thought that he had been the one to cause it made his spine tingle. His spent cock didn't even twitch, but Niall was nonetheless surprised by the pure want Ethan evoked in him.

Ethan grinned, pressing his lips against Niall's and sweeping his tongue into Niall's obliging mouth. Niall sucked at it, enjoying the lazy kiss and the way it made his slowing heart speed again.

Ethan broke away after a minute with a sigh, and it wasn't until then that Niall remembered Ethan's appointment. It was already half past one, which meant if Ethan's 2:00 p.m. meeting was anywhere other than here in his house, he was going to be late.

"Now I need to hurry," Ethan murmured hoarsely against his lips, stealing another quick kiss before standing fully and stretching again, the way his muscles moved under his tanned skin making Niall's mouth go dry. "I need to catch a shower."

Niall started to stand, but Ethan bent again, pushing him back into the chair as he kissed him.

"I won't be able to hurry if you join me," Ethan murmured, and Niall nipped at Ethan's lip in retaliation. "Nothing says we can't take another one after I get home."

Niall laughed and released him, watching as Ethan kicked out the rest of the way out of the boxers pooled around his ankles and half jogged in the direction of the master suite's large bathroom.

"Make yourself at home. I won't be gone more than an hour or so." He disappeared through the french doors, popping his head back out a second later. "We can have that shower, then go out when I get back, have an early dinner."

"Yes, fine! Just go!" Niall laughed when it was clear Ethan didn't intend to move until he had agreed.

SEVENTEEN

NIALL CONSIDERED going back to bed after he'd finally shooed Ethan out the door, but it seemed ridiculous to sleep away the rest of the afternoon, especially since he'd already had a lengthy nap. Ethan had told him to make himself at home, and Niall knew he was alone in the house, since Ethan had given Hortensia a few days off as an apology for the scene she'd walked in on in the foyer.

He stretched his shoulders to get the kinks out, deciding to go downstairs to the kitchen to see if he could find a bag to wrap around his cast so he could grab a shower. He felt gritty and dirty, though he'd showered in the guest room before they'd gone out the night before. He sniffed at his shoulder, wrinkling his nose at the faint scent of hospital antiseptic that still clung to his skin. He definitely needed a shower.

There was a neat pile of pajamas on the bureau. He figured Ethan had probably put them out for him the previous night, intending to have him use them before Niall had fallen asleep so soundly. He scooped them up with his good arm and put them on, then darted into Ethan's bathroom to steal the robe hanging on the back of the door before venturing out into the hallway and down the stairs in search of a plastic bag he could knot around his hand. The doctors had told him short showers were alright as long as he didn't get the plaster wet.

It didn't feel right to use Ethan's bathroom, even after he'd slept in Ethan's bed. It seemed too intimate to simply assume he could use it. Instead, Niall went back to the guest room he'd used the night he'd arrived, using the toiletries he'd found in there yesterday to take a quick shower.

Getting dressed afterward without help had been a dicey proposition, but Niall had managed it reasonably well. Someone had brought in his laundered clothes at some point, since Niall found them neatly pressed and hanging on the closet door. The buttons had taken some doing, but twenty minutes later, he was reasonably put together and standing in Ethan's kitchen, at a loss for what to do with himself.

Wandering through Ethan's house seemed awkward and intrusive, but he was sure Ethan wouldn't mind if he poked around to find something to entertain himself with. Niall hadn't brought any books or magazines with him, but he was sure Ethan must have a library. In his real estate experience, it was rare a home as big as Ethan's didn't have a dedicated library. The owners almost always let the decorator have free reign in there, even if they didn't read for recreation. He was sure there was a room with books somewhere, regardless of whether Ethan had ever cracked the spine on any of them.

After a few wrong turns, he found it, grinning to himself as he passed through the arched doorway into a room filled with sunlight and floor-to-ceiling bookshelves. Either Ethan or his decorator had great taste. Niall had no problem finding a book that caught his interest. He decided to stay in the cozy library, settling into a comfortable chair near the window to read.

An hour later, Ethan still hadn't come back. Niall stood and stretched, marking his place in the book and tucking it under his arm. He was thirsty, but he wasn't sure what Ethan's stance on eating and drinking in the library was. Niall figured he'd move to the kitchen with his book, maybe taking advantage of the comfortable nook he'd noticed the first night. He'd seen plenty of sodas and beers in the small refrigerator under the counter when he'd been looking for a bag for his cast. It had been a bit of a relief that all of the beer had been American brands. He didn't know what he'd do if he found Ethan stocked Guinness.

Niall hadn't bothered with shoes when he'd gotten dressed, and he'd already slipped several times on the slick tile floor. He stumbled as he came out of the library, his good hand scrambling against the archway as he tried to keep his balance. The book fell to the floor and skidded across the hallway into an alcove. Niall bent to retrieve it after he'd regained his balance, nearly knocking his head on the underside of a shelf when he stood.

And suddenly, still a bit disoriented from his near fall, Niall found himself face-to-face with a photo of Ethan in full combat fatigues in a group of soldiers. Their heads were thrown back in laughter, but even obscured like that, there was no mistaking the man Ethan had his arm around. It was Nolan.

At first Niall thought he must have been hallucinating—a side effect of the pain medication, maybe. He sat on the floor, back pressed firmly against the wall to ground himself, and breathed through the worst of the nausea before working up the courage to stand up and look at the picture again.

It hadn't changed in the five minutes he'd been having his mini panic attack. It really was Nolan, with Ethan's arm slung around his shoulders. They were in Afghanistan, that much was obvious from their dusty camouflage uniforms and the scrub-covered hills around them, but there was no clue as to when the picture had been taken. Niall let out a semihysterical laugh as he studied the picture. Did it really matter when Ethan and Nolan had been in Afghanistan together? The important thing was that they had known each other—and well, from the looks of the picture.

Rational thought was slow to return, but after a few minutes rooted there with his heart pounding wildly in his throat, Niall realized he was still standing in Ethan's hallway. The possibility of Ethan walking through the door any moment made his stomach lurch, and that made Niall burst into motion, scrambling back down the hallway without much thought as to where he would go. He ended up in the library, leaning against the windowsill as he considered his options. Niall knew it was cowardly, but he couldn't even contemplate seeing Ethan until he'd settled down. He either had to find himself a hotel until he could think straight or get the next flight out of Seattle.

Every minute that passed was a minute Ethan was closer to returning, so Niall decided the best thing he could do would be to put some distance between himself and Ethan's house. He hadn't brought anything particularly important in his satchel, so he chose the most expedient path of abandoning anything that wasn't already in it and simply grabbing his shoes and booking himself a cab, offering the company a twenty-dollar bonus if the driver was there in ten minutes or less.

He was ready in five, despite the frustration of not being able to put his socks on with the cast complicating matters. After a few aborted tries, he'd simply shoved his feet into his shoes without them.

His mind was whirling so fast he was nearly sick with it. The image of Nolan smiling at him from Ethan's shelf was burned into his brain. Niall couldn't wrap his head around it. Ethan had never mentioned being a soldier. He'd never mentioned he'd known Nolan.

Niall's chest clenched. Could Ethan have possibly known? Had Ethan had sex with him out of pity? He'd been shocked earlier when Niall had told him he hadn't slept with anyone since Nolan had died, but that hadn't been until after he and Ethan had slept together. None of it made sense.

The doorbell rang, and Niall grabbed his satchel, stuffing his socks into his pocket. His shoes weren't tied, but he doubted the cab driver would notice, let alone care.

THE CAB driver had wanted a destination, and Niall had panicked at the question. He'd ended up blurting out the name of a coffee shop

160

he and Clare had gone to the day before. Instead of calling the airport to book a flight as he'd intended, he'd found himself dialing her and asking her to meet him. Fifteen minutes later, he was sitting in a wrought iron chair under a bright-yellow awning, fingers wrapped around a steaming latte he didn't remember ordering.

"Caffeine isn't good for you, you know."

Niall started at the cheery voice, managing a weak smile when Clare slid into the chair next to his.

"Not that I'm not thrilled you called—I am. But you were pretty cryptic on the phone. Feel like telling me why we're here?"

Niall sighed, staring blankly at the diamond pattern on the table. He didn't protest when Clare's battered water bottle appeared under his nose, simply taking it and using it to wash down the small capsule she'd placed in his casted hand.

"Let me guess. More St. John's wort?"

Clare laughed. "An Ativan, actually."

Niall's head snapped up, his mouth hanging open as he gaped at her. "You gave me prescription anxiety medication? What if I had an allergy?"

"It was actually passionflower, which is good for headaches. You were rubbing your temples when I walked up, so I figured it was a safe bet." She shrugged. "Snapped you out of your funk, though."

"Nice."

Clare grinned, and this time Niall found himself returning it with a genuine smile. It faltered a bit when she placed a hand over his uninjured one, squeezing his fingers gently. "What happened to your hand?"

Niall looked down at the cast. He'd forgotten about it, actually. It throbbed dully, but he hadn't grabbed his pain medication on his desperate flight from Ethan's house.

"It's nothing. I had a spill last night. That's not what's wrong."

Clare fixed him with a stern look that told Niall a broken bone wasn't something she considered nothing, but she let it go.

"Alright, let's try that again. What's going on? I thought you and Ethan made up."

Niall suppressed the urge to laugh at the absolute absurdity of the situation. It seemed so outlandish that he was reluctant to tell Clare, but it was true.

"We did. Things are going really well. But I found out something that's going to change everything, and I need some distance from Ethan while I figure things out. He's going to want distance when he finds out what it is too."

Clare squeezed his fingers again, leaning in comfortingly. Niall surprised himself by scooting closer. He'd never been a very tactile person, but something about Clare was soothing.

"What is it Ethan is going to find out?"

Niall had given Clare the bare bones of his life story on the plane, so he was sure she'd understand when he blurted out the problem.

"He knew Nolan."

Clare's mouth dropped open. She clearly hadn't been expecting anything like that. "He told you he knew Nolan?"

"No." Niall toyed with his coffee cup, avoiding eye contact. "There was a picture of the two of them. They served together in Afghanistan."

She was quiet for a moment as she processed. Niall chanced a look up, knowing there was no way Clare was going to let him off this easily without questioning him further.

"What did Ethan say about it? Is he as freaked out as you are?"

Niall bit his lip. "He's at work. I saw the picture after he'd left, and I didn't stick around."

"You left? Just like he left you without a word on the island?"

The irony of the situation wasn't lost on Niall, but it sounded so much worse when Clare said it out loud.

"Yes, but I'm not leaving him without a word. I'm going to call him from the airport to explain." Niall held a hand up when Clare opened her mouth to interrupt. "I'm not leaving for good. I just want to get some space between us for a few days before we talk about it. I'm heading back to Newark to stay with Stephanie until I can clear my head a little."

Clare nodded reluctantly. "That seems like it might be a good idea. As long as you call him, Niall. I'm serious. You need to let him know why you left and make it clear you're not blowing him off."

"He might not want to date me after he finds out. I told him a little bit about Nolan, but it'll be different when Ethan realizes he actually knew him."

There was more to the story of their relationship and Nolan's death, and Niall knew he needed to tell Ethan everything. If Nolan and Ethan were close—and the photo made it look like they were, even though Niall had no memory of Nolan ever talking about anyone named Ethan—then it was likely Ethan would be disgusted by him and wouldn't want to continue their relationship.

"That is, if he doesn't already know. Do you think he did this on purpose?" Niall couldn't keep his voice steady. The thought of Ethan finding him out of some sense of duty to Nolan had his stomach churning.

"No, I really don't." Clare sighed and took her phone out of her purse. "You call Ethan, and I'll call the airline to try to get you on a flight to Newark, alright? He's probably already noticed you're missing, and you don't want him to worry."

Niall hadn't thought about that. He pulled his phone out of his pocket, steeling himself for an unpleasant conversation. Niall hated to admit it, but he was relieved when the call went straight to voicemail; Ethan must still be in his meeting.

He left Ethan a short message, telling him Nolan's full name and that he'd seen the picture hanging outside the library of Ethan and Nolan together. Niall didn't want to go into too much detail until he was able to think things through, so he closed with a brief explanation that he needed some time to himself and a promise he'd let Ethan know when he landed in Newark.

Clare was still on her phone, jotting down flight information on the back of a receipt. She pushed it across the table after she hung up.

"I still don't think you should leave. You can even crash at my place if you don't want to stay with him."

There weren't any direct flights to Newark, but Niall could catch one headed to Denver that left in two hours and make it onto a flight to New Jersey from there.

"It's more than just the two of them being friends, Clare." Niall stuffed the receipt into his pocket and fiddled with his coffee cup again, full of nervous energy. "I have a lot to think about, and it's going to be easier to have the conversation with Ethan if we aren't face-to-face."

Easier for Ethan to walk away was what Niall meant, but he knew if he told her that she'd insist he stay.

"Can you get me to the airport?"

"Of course." She looked down, her lips curving into a smile. "If you promise to call me when you land in Newark, I'll even tie your shoes for you."

NIALL DIDN'T call Stephanie until he was already waiting for his flight to board at the airport. Clare had gotten most of the story out of him on the drive to the airport. It had been easy to tell her the things he'd never be able to confess to Steph, like that he'd slept with Ethan and thought he was falling in love with him. Clare had been sympathetic and supportive, and Niall had been a bit sad when she'd left him at the Delta terminal after seeing him safely inside. Of all of the unlikely things that had happened to him over the last few days, forming what seemed like a true friendship over the span of a cross-country flight was definitely up there. Of course, it wasn't as unlikely as finding out his new love interest had apparently been good friends with his dead partner.

Sighing in resignation, Niall picked up his phone and dialed Stephanie. She'd never forgive him if he didn't tell her what had happened. Besides, he needed her to pick him up in Newark. There was nothing for it. He'd have to rehash the mortifying turn of events yet again.

Her response was exactly what he'd expected—and eerily similar to Clare's. Stephanie had exclaimed over the would-be mugging and questioned him until she was sure he was alright, broken wrist aside, before she'd launched into a diatribe about giving Ethan a chance to explain himself before running away.

Niall had spent most of his adult life in a relationship with Nolan, and it seemed like the only other relationship he'd ever had, no matter how short-lived, somehow involved Nolan too. Niall was at a loss for how to function now he'd found someone else, opened himself up to falling in love again, and then had Nolan thrust into the middle of it. Would he never escape the guilt he felt about Nolan? Part of him knew he'd moved to Tortola not only to feel closer to Nolan but also to avoid putting himself out there and finding love with someone new.

Part of Niall still worried Stephanie would be angry Niall was falling for someone other than her brother, but she'd been over the moon at the news that he thought he'd found someone he could fall in love with again. Niall was chagrined to have to admit she'd been right all along, that paying off his boat had been Ethan's way of admitting he had feelings for Niall and not some passive-aggressive way of paying him off. Though who knew if that was actually true— maybe he'd known the truth all along and paid the boat off out of loyalty to Nolan. Not that Steph would let him rant about that.

"So you're not even going to try? You're just going to run away like he did?"

Niall had balked when she'd said it, but the words rang true now as he thought about the conversation, slumped in the uncomfortable airplane seat. Was he making a mistake? It felt like he'd been living in a vacuum ever since Nolan's death, first escaping the memories they'd made together in Hull by fleeing to the States, then by uprooting his entire life and moving to Tortola. It was almost as if he'd been in some sort of emotional stasis for the past few years, frozen in his grief and regret, until Ethan had appeared and turned the lonely world he'd made for himself upside down.

He couldn't tell Stephanie why the fact that Ethan had known Nolan was so important. It would have meant confessing his darkest secret to her, and he couldn't risk doing that. He'd already lost Nolan, though in truth he was fairly certain he'd lost at least part of him even before he'd died. Still, he couldn't stand to lose Stephanie, Roger, and Camille, especially after falling for Ethan so quickly and having it all come crumbling down around his ears.

NIALL FELT like a robot as he shuffled forward, following the line of people out of the plane. They'd landed in Denver, and he had an hour's layover before his flight to Newark. Enough time to call Ethan and explain why he'd left. He wouldn't leave Ethan wondering and worrying like he had when Ethan had been the one pulling the disappearing act. Niall owed him that much at the very least.

He was fumbling with his gate pass, trying to figure out where he had to go next, when he heard someone call his name. He looked up, confused, and saw a lanky man in a leather jacket and jeans waving him over.

"Niall Ahern?"

Niall nodded, wondering who he could be. He didn't look like an airline official or airport security.

"There's been a change in your flight plan. If you'll come with me, I'll walk you down to your new gate." Niall stared at him, and the man grimaced.

"Sorry. Joe Dennison," he said, holding out his hand. Niall shifted his satchel to his right shoulder, reaching out awkwardly with his left hand to shake it.

"I don't understand. I'm booked on Delta," Niall said, looking over Joe's shoulder at the airline clerk who was standing behind the ticket counter at the gate he'd just come from.

"I spoke with Stephanie. Your sister?"

Niall's frown deepened. He'd given Stephanie his flight information so she could pick him up at the airport in Newark. Had she changed his flight?

"Sister-in-law," he said automatically. It was a common mistake among people who hadn't known Nolan, though Niall didn't have many friends to make the assumption anyway. "Wait, Stephanie called?"

Joe nodded. "If you'll just come with me, it'll all be clear in a few minutes."

Niall pulled out his cell phone, scowling at Joe as he dialed. Stephanie picked up on the first ring, as if she'd been expecting his call.

"You changed my flight?" he asked without preamble.

Niall hurried to keep up with Joe's long strides as Stephanie explained she'd found him a better flight that would get him home faster. He didn't bother arguing with her. It was a pure Stephanie move.

"I'll see you soon," Niall said after she'd finished.

"Sure, talk to you in a bit. Love you!" Stephanie answered, ending the call before Niall could return the sentiment.

He looked at the phone, puzzled by her odd behavior, before shoving it back into his pocket and looking at Joe.

"Do you have any other bags we need to worry about?" Joe asked, offering to take the satchel still looped around Niall's shoulder. Niall waved him off, unwilling to give up what little control over the situation he had left.

"Stephanie said I was flying a different airline?"

Joe nodded, stopping at airport security to show a badge of some sort. Niall relaxed a bit— he wasn't wearing a uniform, but he must be some sort of airport personnel. The security guard opened the door with a key card and let them through. Niall blinked when he realized they were walking down a corridor like the type used during boarding.

"Is this my flight?" he asked, but Joe only sped up, walking faster until they reached the end of the hallway. Instead of being hooked up to an airplane, though, Niall was surprised to see stairs leading out onto the tarmac.

"I really think there must be a mistake," he said, feeling uneasy.

"No mistake. Your plane is this way," Joe said, heading down the stairs and outside. Niall followed, squinting as the sun reflected off the planes. They were all small, like private jets. Before Niall could protest again, Joe stopped in front of a sleek Cessna that didn't look remotely like anything Delta would fly.

But it wasn't the jet that had Niall's jaw dropping. It was the person standing at the bottom of the stairs. Ethan.

EIGHTEEN

"I DIDN'T think you'd come if I was the one who met your plane," Ethan said simply, hands tucked into his pockets.

Niall looked back at Joe, who seemed distinctly uncomfortable.

"Joe's my pilot. Don't blame him. He gets paid to do my bidding."

Joe rolled his eyes.

"We should be ready in about twenty minutes." He stepped past Ethan, who moved to the side to let him slide by.

"I'm not going anywhere with you." Niall didn't care how brittle and petty his voice sounded. He turned around, prepared to go back the way he'd come, only to see that the door they'd come through had no handle on the outside. "I told you I needed some time."

"Just come in and talk. If you still want to fly to Newark, I'll have Joe take you there."

Niall pursed his lips. "You called Stephanie?"

Ethan shook his head. "Stephanie called me, and so did a woman named Clare Smith. Neither of them had my cell number, but luckily Susannah was still at the office answering the main line."

Niall pressed his lips into a grim line. He wasn't entirely surprised both women had tried to intervene on his behalf. He didn't know whether to be angry with them or grateful. After all, he'd been planning to call Ethan again during his layover. Would it really be that much harder to tell him what he needed to in person? Niall snorted softly, shaking his head. Of course it would be—that had been the whole reason he'd left.

"I'll come up, but just to talk," Niall said slowly, watching Ethan carefully.

Ethan gave Niall a shuttered look but nodded, starting up the stairs. Niall hesitated for a moment and followed him.

"Drink?" Ethan asked as they stepped into the interior of the plane. Niall couldn't believe the opulence: leather seats twice as big as the one he'd been wedged into on the flight from Seattle, glossy console tables, and thick, plush carpet that felt softer underfoot than the carpet in most homes.

Niall shook his head, feeling guilty. Ethan must have dropped everything to come after him. It made him feel like an idiot.

"Alright," Ethan said quietly, slumping into a chair. It was the first time Niall had seen him with anything other than near-perfect posture. It hurt his heart a little to see Ethan look so despondent and know he was the cause.

Niall considered remaining standing to keep some distance between them, but his exhaustion got the best of him and he sat in the chair next to Ethan's, not wanting to sit across from him because he didn't want to have to look him in the eye.

"So you knew Nolan."

Ethan nodded, his mouth set in a grim line. "Pretty well. But before we get into that, you probably want these."

He put the bottle of pills Niall had forgotten on the table between them, producing a bottle of water to go with it. Without a word, Ethan shook two pills out into his palm and offered them to Niall, then unscrewed the water bottle's lid for him as well.

The thoughtfulness of the action made Niall's chest hurt. Ethan obviously cared about him and wanted to take care of him. He took the pills, nodding his thanks after washing them down with the water.

"I wasn't really thinking clearly when I left," he said sheepishly as Ethan put the bottles away.

"I figured. Your message was pretty panicked. I was worried about you."

"It was a pretty big shock." Niall wondered if he'd ever said anything that was as much of an understatement as that one sentence. It had been more than a shock; it had tipped his world on its axis, and things still hadn't settled. Niall leaned forward when Ethan made no move speak, but Ethan waved for him to wait and disappeared into a small closet near the front of the plane's passenger area, coming back with two crystal glasses and a bottle of Glenlivet. He set them on the console table between the two seats, uncapping the bottle and pouring two generous fingers of the amber liquid into the glasses.

Niall's head felt like it had been stuffed with cotton wool, but he figured it was likely due more to the emotional upheaval than the pain medication he'd just taken, so he threw caution to the wind, fumbling the heavy cut-crystal tumbler a bit with his left hand as he lifted it awkwardly to his mouth and took a sip.

Niall coughed as the alcohol burned a path down his throat. He could feel it pool in his stomach, spreading warmth through his belly. He couldn't help but make a face as the expensive scotch's aftertaste coated his tongue, and Ethan laughed sharply, taking a deep drink out of his own glass without so much as a sputter or wince.

"I can't say I blame you for running," Ethan said after he swallowed. "Oh, I was livid. For the first ten minutes or so, I could hardly see straight. Susannah insisted on driving me to the airport herself because she was afraid of what I'd do behind the wheel."

Niall bent his head, chagrined. He'd been absolutely furious when Ethan had left Tortola without a word, and here he'd done the exact same thing to him. That he'd meant to explain later didn't make it any better. Ethan had had the same intentions, after all, and look at how that had turned out.

"Then I stopped and really thought about it. Niall, Jesus. I can't even begin to understand how you must have felt when you saw the picture." Ethan slipped a hand over Niall's on the armrest and Niall made no move to dislodge it. "I didn't know. I swear to God, I didn't know."

Niall nodded gracelessly. He felt almost numb, which was a welcome relief from the roller coaster ride his emotions had been on all day. His head felt light, and he realized the headache that had been thrumming behind his temples was all but gone. Suddenly mixing alcohol with the painkillers didn't seem like such a good idea. He didn't know if the lurching in his belly was due to that or to having Ethan there in front of him, but it was disconcerting all the same.

"I overreacted. It's not rational, I know. I'm sorry for leaving like that," Niall said, swallowing hard.

"Niall, God." Ethan blew out a breath, shaking his head. "I've never really met anyone before who I clicked with like I did with you. And things were going so well, and then I came out of my meeting and had that voicemail from you."

Niall didn't respond, giving Ethan the chance to get everything off his chest.

"Your message was a shock. I was as blindsided by it as you were. But then I thought about it, and suddenly it made sense, you know? Little things, like your refrigerator being empty of just about everything but Guinness, which I know was his favorite beer. I used to tease him about it. I've always hated it. I told him I thought it tasted like a beer milkshake."

Niall laughed humorlessly, knowing how much the jab would have bothered Nolan. It felt good in a way to reminisce about Nolan like this. Painful, but good.

"I was a Marine. I met him during my second tour in Afghanistan. I'd joined right after high school, mostly because my father expected I'd go straight to college." Ethan smiled at the memory. "I found I enjoyed it, though. That's why I signed up for the second tour after I finished the first. Nolan and I were both reconnaissance specialists. We went on a lot of the same missions, and we got to know each other."

Niall remained silent, staring down at his knees.

"We hung out whenever we could. He had a wicked sense of humor I loved, and he was always telling jokes. He used to say I was too pretty to be a Marine. He called me—"

"Betty," Niall finished for him as everything clicked into place. "He called you Betty."

Ethan nodded slowly, features taut with tension. His usually sparkling eyes held a haunted quality Niall knew well. He'd seen it on Nolan's face whenever he'd talked about friends he'd lost.

Niall had heard stories about Betty. It had been years and years ago, but he still remembered the name popping up in many of Nolan's letters home. Betty, who had a great head for computers. Betty, who had helped Nolan prank his commanding officer more than once. Betty, who had stopped Nolan from entering a building seconds before it had blown up.

"You saved his life once," Niall said, his mind whirling. Was he ever going to be over Nolan? How could he get over him if reminders of him kept popping up? When he'd first met Ethan, he'd given himself permission to do what he wanted to do instead of what he thought Nolan would have wanted him to do for the first time since Nolan's death. And now here he was again, buried in guilt and letting Nolan shape his life, even in death.

"I'm surprised he told you. He told everyone else he'd saved my ass." Ethan's tone was dry, sarcastic, but his face showed none of the amusement Niall had come to associate with him. He looked up, meeting Niall's eye. "He was a great guy. We kept up through e-mail for a few years after I left the service, but then the software company took off and I got busy with other things. The e-mails trailed off to every few months and then once a year and then, after he never responded to my last one, I just figured he'd moved on."

Niall felt like his face was numb. He couldn't tell if he was frowning or not.

"It happens. I know a lot of guys who kind of shut the door on their time in the service after they returned to civilian life. It's—it's a lot to deal with, readjusting. I know Nolan had been having some trouble. So I figured when I stopped hearing from him that he'd, I don't know. Decided to cut ties, I guess."

"He had been having some trouble readjusting to civilian life, but he was still in touch with everyone. He used to give me updates from your e-mails. The day before he died, he told me about some big software deal Betty had closed," Niall said quietly.

"I saw a picture of you once. You had a hat on and a huge pair of sunglasses, or I might have recognized you on Tortola. Gennie had his arm wrapped around you, and the two of you were grinning your faces off on the deck of some sloop."

Gennie. Niall had managed to forget that tidbit of Nolan's life. Most of his friends had called him Gentry, since it wasn't uncommon for marines to go by their last names. But to get back at Nolan for nicknaming him Betty, Ethan had shortened it to Gennie instead. Niall took a loud breath, the sound startling in the otherwise quiet cabin. He didn't like dredging up all these old memories, but there was a different quality to them now. He was sharing them with someone who'd known Nolan. It felt—good. The horrible emptiness that usually made him feel so hollow when he thought about Nolan wasn't there, replaced by a slight ache that felt like a sore muscle getting stretched the day after a good workout.

"The reason I was in Tortola was because Nolan had told me he had a home there. He said it was the only place he could imagine retiring. He used to tell us stories about the island and the great fishing there. The beautiful sunsets, the perfect weather. When I decided I wanted a vacation home, I immediately thought about him and Tortola."

Niall didn't know what to say. His past and his present were all wrapped up together in one big, emotional mess and he was at a loss for how to react. At every turn, it seemed like Nolan was there.

Ethan seemed to sense Niall was overwhelmed. He busied himself pouring another shot into his own glass, not bothering to top off Niall's tumbler.

"He said his partner's name was Nil. I had no idea, Niall, I promise. All I know is when I walked into the terminal and saw you standing there talking to the taxi driver in your completely inappropriate wool suit, you intrigued me. And then you opened your mouth and started babbling in that accent of yours, and I was absolutely lost. Do you have any idea how gorgeous you are, Niall? How completely charming you are, or how endearing I find your awkwardness?"

Niall bristled a bit, narrowing his eyes as he studied Ethan. But there was nothing but open honesty on Ethan's face.

"You were just so different from the kind of men I usually meet. I wanted desperately to get to know you, but short of withdrawing as your client, I knew there was nothing I could do to get past your shell. So I took a chance and told you I'd made arrangements to stay with you, even though I hadn't."

"You what?" Niall's sputter of outrage made Ethan's lips twist into a grin, making him look ten years younger.

"I knew if I let you take me to a hotel, I'd only see you for showings, and there was no way I'd get you to open up. So I called my secretary and screamed at her for a few minutes. You have no idea how much groveling it took to get Susannah to forgive me, by the way. It involved a box from Tiffany's."

Before a few days ago, it would have been hard to imagine Ethan groveling to anyone. But Niall had seen it firsthand when

Ethan had been apologizing to Hortensia, and Niall laughed despite himself. Ethan's smile grew at the sound.

"So I basically forced you to take me home with you. Dinner that night—Niall, I swear, it was the best date I'd had in years, and you didn't even know it was a date."

Niall felt suddenly, inexplicably shy. He looked down, studying the glass of scotch his hand was still curled around. He used to like scotch. And whiskey. Even brandy. But he'd gotten out of the habit of drinking anything but Guinness since Nolan died.

"I should have known. The clues were all there. Where you're from, the beer, the name of the boat—yeah, Nolan told me about what Orion meant to you two."

Niall's chest clenched. It had been their secret, and Nolan sharing it with someone else stung. His hurt must have been obvious, because Ethan hurried to explain.

"He didn't mean to break your confidence, I don't think. I'd caught him stargazing about a dozen times before he finally admitted why. It was a beautiful gesture, Niall. And Nolan, he looked for it every chance he got. He loved you so much."

It felt both comforting and awkward to have Ethan reassuring him how much Nolan loved him. On one hand, he'd spent the last few years trying to be worthy of the love Nolan had given him because he'd felt so guilty about resenting him after he'd come home. Part of him would always love Nolan, though, and hearing that Nolan had thought about him often while he'd been stationed overseas, even to the point of telling his friends, meant a lot. But on the other hand, if Niall wanted any possibility of having a relationship with Ethan, they both had to get past Nolan, and having Ethan talk about him wasn't helping matters.

"We almost met once, you know. Gennie invited me to come visit him. He wanted to take me sailing and get me 'a proper beer.'" Ethan looked almost apologetic, the words soft and hesitant.

"I know." Niall smiled ruefully. He'd been furious with Nolan about it at the time. Niall blinked, remembering the screaming match they'd had when Nolan had announced a friend would be staying with them during the two-week furlough, the first time they'd seen each other in almost a year. He remembered Nolan planning a pub crawl through Hull so he could introduce Betty to the wonders of a properly pulled ale.

"He said you hated Guinness because you were an ugly American, but he didn't hold it against you because you didn't know any better," Niall said quietly, taking a shaky breath.

Betty had canceled at the last minute because his father had died, and Betty had gone home for the funeral and to settle his estate. Niall remembered Nolan telling him how devastated Betty had been by the loss. "I'm sorry about your father."

Ethan shot him a sad smile and nodded.

"He wanted to show you off too. He was always talking about you. Like I said, he never called you Niall. I probably would have put two and two together earlier if he had," Ethan said with a wry smile.

"Nolan never called me that. We were small when we met, and Nolan couldn't pronounce Niall properly back then, so he called me Nil. It caught on, and everyone in his family called me that," Niall said softly.

"Nolan told me how much you hated the idea of living on the island and running a fishing charter, which is another reason I didn't connect you two in my mind after we'd met," Ethan said, and Niall's heart felt like it had stopped in his chest, replaced by hot, bubbling panic. Had Nolan known his true feelings about their plans for the future? He'd been so careful not to trample on Nolan's ambitions. He'd tried so hard to be a good partner, a good friend.

"What? No. No, I—"

Ethan's hand closed over Niall's, squeezing until he released his grip on the glass. Ethan threaded their fingers together, the gentle pressure grounding Niall in the present and saving him from his internal panic.

"He never intended to make you move to the island," Ethan said, and Niall's entire body stiffened. "We all did things like that while we were deployed. It helped to while away the lonely hours if you could fantasize about what your life would be like after the service. Nolan took his love of boats and turned it into an elaborate fantasy about running a fishing charter with you. I fantasized about telling my father I wasn't going to get an MBA and join his company as an accountant."

Niall's fingers were lax in Ethan's, but Ethan didn't release them.

"But you didn't do that. You started a degree in computer science at MIT but left without finishing it after the software you created started selling."

Niall blushed a bit as Ethan looked at him incredulously. Given the Google searches Niall had done on Ethan, both before and after meeting him, there wasn't much of Ethan's professional history he didn't know by heart.

"Because my father died and his partners bought out my mother's share of the business," Ethan said with a shrug. "So suddenly it wasn't an unreachable fantasy. But that's not what it was for Nolan, Niall. He always thought he'd get a job managing the sailing club and the two of you would use the house he bought on Tortola as a vacation home. He used to tell me that when you two were old and gray, maybe you'd tire of the weather in England and you'd live on the island full time."

"I thought he was just biding his time at the sailing club. He was doing odd jobs for them, never going after any real job. I just thought—I thought he wasn't going to be happy unless we followed through on his plan."

Ethan smiled grimly, gripping Niall's hand harder. "There were a hundred reasons why the charter wouldn't work, and Nolan knew them all. So did you, because he told me you were always the practical one, thinking everything through." Ethan brought Niall's hand up to his mouth, kissing his fingers softly. "I was so jealous of him. You kept him so grounded, you loved him so much. I wanted that. It's never something I've had, not with any of my lovers. And when I met you, I thought to myself, 'I could see myself falling in love with him.' And then I did fall, just a little, the night we spent on the boat." Ethan gave a self-deprecating laugh, shaking his head. "That's why I paid off the Orion's mortgage. It seemed fitting."

"Even after you thought I was carousing with all those other men?" Niall couldn't quite hold back his teasing tone, and Ethan gave him a look of mock consternation. "We never did talk about that, you know. I know you fancy yourself a—what did you call yourself? A knight in shining armor? How did you even know where to go to pay off my loan?"

Ethan looked abashed. "I didn't. I just had my financial advisor put in calls to all the major banks and found it that way."

Niall gaped. "That sounds illegal."

"Probably was."

"But that would have been after you called the office and concluded I was sleeping around already. Why would you still have paid Orion off? You wouldn't even return my calls by that point."

"I never said it was rational," Ethan said, grinning. "Even if you had been the Casanova I'd taken you for, it didn't change how I felt about you."

"So you'd pay off a $400,000 loan but not return a call?"

Ethan shrugged.

"It doesn't—" Niall wanted to say it doesn't matter now, but he found the words sticking in his throat. It did matter. Ethan had said he'd fallen a little bit in love with Niall after those first few days. Would he still be when he found out more about how Nolan died? Because though Niall desperately wanted for it not to be true, Niall knew he could definitely fall head over heels for Ethan.

He just wasn't sure they could make it work, with their shared past. Or rather, with Nolan as their shared past. Niall knew if he didn't get the entire story out now he might never be able to, and it was definitely something Ethan needed to know if they were going to try to be together.

He'd given Ethan the bare bones of the story the night before in the ER, but he hadn't been able to bring himself to fill in the details. But now, Niall needed to tell Ethan everything—the things he hadn't told Stephanie, Mrs. Jim, or even the therapist Stephanie had insisted Niall see.

"There's more," Niall said, gathering his courage. He hoped Ethan wouldn't interrupt; Niall wasn't sure he could start again if Ethan stopped him. "Last night, it was just too much. When I saw you arguing with that man, it was like what happened to Nolan all over again."

Ethan looked at him silently, his face full of compassion.

"I wasn't there when Nolan died, but there was a police report. It was—" Niall's voice broke and he swallowed hard. "It was a lot like what happened last night. He saw a girl getting roughed up by a mugger and tried to help her, but the bastard had a knife and stabbed him. Nolan bled out before they could get him to the emergency room, even though the hospital was only three goddamn blocks away."

He looked up when Ethan hummed unhappily, looking like he wanted to reach out and comfort him. But Niall didn't want that, and he rushed to continue so Ethan would understand. He didn't want the compassion he saw in Ethan's eyes. He didn't deserve it.

Niall's voice was thick with unshed tears but he kept on, determined not to stop until Ethan knew the whole story, including the most damning part. Niall's guilt over his part in Nolan's death had been why he hadn't been able to stay in New Jersey with Stephanie and her family, though she'd begged him to. Niall couldn't look at her every day and live with the fact that she didn't know the truth, but by the same token he couldn't live without some link to Nolan, no matter how tenuous. It was a catch-22; he couldn't stay near her until he'd told her the truth, and if he confessed everything to her she'd never want to see him again.

Ethan hadn't moved, his eyes locked on Niall. It was as if he was trying to be absolutely still in the hopes Niall might forget he had an audience and continue on with his story. The thought made something in Niall's heart twist. Ethan was the only person he could see himself telling the story to. Were it not for his presence, Niall probably wouldn't even be able to say the words out loud in an empty room.

"Nolan was in London, but I'd stayed in Hull. His mother was in the hospital. They'd called earlier and said she'd had a heart attack. He left the minute they called, but I didn't. I told him I had an important showing that evening and I'd join him in the morning, but really, I just didn't want to go. Anne Marie didn't approve of our relationship, and I didn't feel like dealing with her caustic comments. I was so sure she was faking it; it was exactly the kind of thing she did, desperate to get Nolan and Stephanie's attention."

Niall studied his uninjured hand, which was twisted in the fabric of his jacket. He hadn't registered he was still wearing it despite the almost stifling confines of the plane. He'd never told anyone this part, not even his overpriced therapist, but he couldn't stop the words from spilling out of his mouth.

"So I stayed home. He took the train in, because we only had the one car, and if I was showing a house, I'd need it. So he took the train, never complaining about it once. And as he was walking from the station to the hospital, he was stabbed. He died while I was eating fish and chips from the shop down the street and watching East Enders."

Niall laughed bitterly, the sound harsh in the otherwise silent space.

"He hated that show, and I'd gotten addicted to it while he was serving in Afghanistan. We'd fought about it the morning he died, actually. It annoyed him to no end that I'd let them pile up on the DVR and crowd out other recordings until I had a free weekend to watch them all in one go. And I told him sometimes I felt closer to Ian Beale and Ricky Butcher than I did to him, because the show, their characters—they'd never left me for months at a time."

Niall expected Ethan to recoil, but he didn't. Seemingly sensing Niall was unsure about continuing, Ethan slid a hand over Niall's, squeezing his fingers lightly. Niall watched with detached fascination as first one drop and then two of water fell on Ethan's cuff, forming perfect darkened circles on the material. Ethan was still wearing the suit he'd put on when he'd left for his meeting, though the coat was rumpled and unbuttoned.

By the time the third wet circle appeared on Ethan's sleeve, soaking into the fabric and expanding until it blended the other two together, Niall realized he'd started crying at some point in his confession. Silent tears coursed down Niall's face, but he made no move to take his hand out of Ethan's grasp and wipe them away.

"I said horrible things to him that morning, horrible. And he said horrible things to me, as well. And then I went to work, still angry, and he did God only knows what around the house like he did most days when he was between handyman jobs at the club. And then the hospital called, and I was still so angry with him that when he called me to tell me about Anne Marie, I lied and told him I couldn't go."

Niall took a deep breath, his hand twitching under Ethan's. He felt exhausted, wrung out, and suddenly embarrassed. He had no doubt that now Ethan knew the truth he'd want nothing to do with him, and Niall couldn't blame him.

"And then he was killed, and I never got to tell him how much I loved him or how sorry I was that we'd fought."

Niall took a breath, unable to meet Ethan's eyes after his confession.

"I'll just go." Niall pulled his hand out from under Ethan's, pushing up out of the buttery soft leather seat as he did. He didn't want to make a scene, but he needed to get off the plane and back to Stephanie's before he completely broke down.

Except—how could he go to Stephanie's? It was like finally talking about that night had opened up a floodgate inside him, all of the things Niall had disliked about Nolan surging up to the forefront

182

of his mind. It made him feel petty and disgusted with himself. He couldn't face Stephanie until he'd gotten a handle on everything. If he was being honest with himself, which he was, possibly for the first time in years, Niall knew that wasn't about to happen anytime soon.

He'd finally let himself admit he and Nolan hadn't had the perfect relationship. They'd been struggling, no matter how much Niall hated to admit it. He loved Nolan fiercely, but he'd been so frustrated that Nolan hadn't shown any sign of settling into a career once he'd finally retired from the military. It was as if he'd had no ambition outside of the Royal Marines, other than owning a charter company on an island in the middle of godforsaken nowhere.

"Niall!" Ethan jumped to his feet, catching Niall as he tried to edge past Ethan.

"No, it's—I'm sorry. I had no right to unload all that on you, and I'm sorry. I'll—"

Niall made an undignified sound of surprise when Ethan's hand closed around his upper arm, above his elbow, and clamped down tightly. He tripped on the runner in the aisle, his injured hand flailing out for purchase and rapping smartly against the back of one of the seats. Niall hissed out a pained breath, immediately cradling the cast to his chest as he glared weakly at Ethan through bleary eyes.

Ethan pulled him back down into the seat, holding him there with a hand on his thigh. "Niall, don't."

"Don't what?" Niall took a breath and shook his head. "Never mind, it doesn't matter. Just let me go."

"Niall."

Niall looked up, jaw set. He was confused by what he saw in Ethan's eyes. Surely after everything he'd told him, Ethan wouldn't still want anything to do with him. Not only had he admitted he was a horrible person, but Ethan had known Nolan. How could Ethan possibly want to have a relationship with someone as selfish as Niall?

"Ethan, please," Niall begged. He wasn't sure what he was asking of Ethan anymore. Please let him go? Please forgive him for being so fucked up? Please what?

Before he could say anything more, though, Niall found himself pulled forward roughly, Ethan releasing Niall's thigh so he could wrap his arms around him. Niall pressed his face against the smooth skin bared by the few open buttons at Ethan's neck, breathing in his warm, spicy scent and taking comfort from the familiarity of it. He'd done something similar two nights ago, and it was scary how quickly Ethan's scent had become ingrained with safety and comfort in Niall's mind. It made him feel safe even though he felt like the world was pitching around him, like it had when he'd nestled close to Ethan months earlier, clinging to him as a hurricane rocked the Orion.

"I should be apologizing to you." Ethan's words were quiet, but in the buzzing silence of the plane's interior, Niall heard them perfectly clearly. "You tried to stop me last night, and I didn't listen. If I had, we would have avoided the whole mess."

"I thought I might lose you the same way I lost Nolan, and it scared the shit out of me, Ethan."

Ethan flinched back a bit but nodded. "I can't promise I'll never get hurt, Niall."

Niall nodded, blinking to try to dispel the hot prick of tears before they took hold and started to fall again. "I've been lost since Nolan died," he said, his voice breaking on Nolan's name. "And then you came along and I felt something I hadn't in a long time."

Ethan nodded, pinching the bridge of his nose and taking a breath. Niall looked up, shocked by the obvious display of emotion.

"And then I didn't listen to you and got in the middle of what we thought was a fight, and you saw Nolan's death happening all over again, right?"

Niall made a broken sound and looked down.

"Listen, it's alright. Okay, Niall? What you're feeling? It's okay. No one should lose someone the way you lost Nolan, and that's not going to be something you get over."

Dozens of people had said the exact same thing to him, but the words sounded different coming from Ethan. Or maybe he was finally in a place he was ready to hear them, Niall thought. "Yeah."

Niall found himself enveloped in a hug. Ethan's arms wrapped around him tighter, pulling him close and holding him there as Niall tried to get control of his emotions. Between talking about Nolan's death, the prescription painkillers, and the scotch, Niall felt strung out and exhausted.

It was hard to wrap his head around the fact that Ethan wasn't asking him to leave. Ethan knew his past. Niall had confessed his darkest, most shameful secret to him, and Ethan hadn't done anything but offer comfort. As broken and battered as he felt by recent happenings, Niall also felt lighter than he had in years.

Niall looked up, fully meeting Ethan's eyes for the first time since he'd seen Ethan at the bottom of the Cessna's stairs. He'd been bewildered and angry to see Ethan at the time, but if Niall was completely honest with himself, he'd also felt relieved. Giddy. Loved. He'd told Ethan before he wasn't a damsel in distress, but part of him liked the rescue, even if it wasn't entirely necessary.

"I don't—" Niall trailed off, words failing him again. There simply weren't any to explain the turmoil he was feeling, or to adequately express his feelings for Ethan.

Ethan watched him silently, and from the expression on his face, Niall could tell he was expecting rejection. Ethan let his hand fall away from Niall's, resting it limply at his side. It was a clear gesture. He wouldn't stop Niall if Niall left.

Instead of leaving, though, Niall surged up in his seat, bridging the gap between them, his good hand braced against the console for balance as he captured Ethan's lips in a hard, desperate kiss. Ethan made a startled noise, too shocked to respond for the first few seconds as Niall's hungry lips roamed over his. He recovered quickly, bringing his arms up to wrap around Niall's shoulders and tug him closer, upsetting the half-full bottle of Glenlivet and sending both it and the glasses falling to the carpeted floor.

"God, I thought... Niall. If you don't... I can't...." Ethan pulled back, resting his forehead against Niall's as he panted for breath. "Please. If this isn't what you want, then I can't. I can't let you walk away from me again. If you're in, you have to be all in. I love you. God help me, but I do."

Niall felt his stomach flip. It took him a minute to realize it wasn't just Ethan's words behind the butterflies. The plane was actually taking off. He could see the clouds through the side windows, blue sky taking up most of the panes as the ground receded below them. He cast a wild glance toward the door, relieved to see that at some point while they'd been otherwise engaged, someone had closed it.

"I'm all in," he whispered against Ethan's lips, his heart hammering in his chest as Ethan stared at him at point-blank range for a long second before dragging him fully across the table and sending both of them tumbling to the scotch-soaked floor.

They slid slightly as the plane tilted, and Ethan's hand shot out to grab the table, which was bolted to the floor, to stop them from rolling more. Niall grimaced when he realized they were both covered in scotch.

"Where are we going?" Niall asked, unbuttoning his outer shirt, which had soaked up most of the alcohol, and shucking it off.

"Home," Ethan said simply. He raised an arm and brushed at the scotch dripping from his coat. His cuff links had a U.S. Marines logo on them Niall hadn't noticed before, and it made Niall want to laugh.

It seemed ridiculously obvious now that Ethan came from a military background. Niall should have been able to spot the signs. Ethan carried himself the same way Nolan had, and Niall could think of dozens of times that stood out in his memory when Ethan had seemed distracted, scanning their surroundings for any potential threat. Nolan had been part of a team that did reconnaissance, and so had Betty. It seemed so strange to think of Ethan as Betty. Niall had gotten to know Betty through the stories Nolan had told about him, and he was finding it wasn't hard at all to merge those memories. It actually felt comforting to know he and Ethan knew each other's histories, though they hadn't talked about a lot of it.

It was a little chilly in the interior of the plane in his thin undershirt and Niall shivered, curling in on himself. He nearly jumped in surprise when Ethan spoke up in a voice only a little louder than normal.

"Joe? Heat in the cabin, please."

"Done, boss."

Niall's eyes widened when the pilot's voice came over the speakers. Had Joe been listening the entire time? Was that how he'd known it was safe to take off? Niall felt an embarrassed flush spread over his cheeks.

"He's discreet," Ethan said quietly, picking up the mostly empty bottle and the two glasses and tucking them into the base of the table, which had a compartment with a tall lip to keep them from rolling away if the plane tilted again. "But yes. He probably heard everything."

"I guess that means no mile-high make-up sex?"

The words had been quiet, but apparently not quite quiet enough.

"We're not quite to a mile high yet, gentlemen. That'll be our cruising height in about—" There was silence as he checked the panels. "—ten minutes."

Ethan laughed, the sound filling Niall with warmth. He hadn't heard Ethan laugh like that since their first night on the island, when they'd had dinner at the curry shop before everything had gotten so complicated.

"Thanks for the heads up, Joe."

Niall bit back a chuckle, worried if he started laughing, he'd never stop. It seemed like his options were laughter or tears, but he wasn't sure the laughter wouldn't end in the latter anyway.

"He can turn off the channel if he wants to," Ethan said, raising his voice again slightly so there was no question of Joe hearing him.

"Don't do anything I wouldn't do, gentlemen. I'll turn it back on to give you a twenty-minute warning before we land," Joe answered, and then there was a loud crackle through the speakers as he closed the connection.

Niall gave in to the giggles, pressing his face against Ethan's shirt and laughing until his stomach ached. It was borderline hysterical, but it felt good to let loose. When he'd settled down, Ethan shifted them so they were cuddled together more comfortably on the seats, with Niall's back to Ethan's broad chest.

"Joe said he'd give us a warning at twenty minutes before we land," Niall murmured, snuggling in closer to Ethan's warmth. "How much time does that leave us?"

"A little less than two hours."

Niall pushed his hands under Ethan's suit coat, urging it off his shoulders as he leaned in and coaxed Ethan into a deep kiss. Ethan cooperated, shrugging out of the coat and letting it pool carelessly on the seat behind them as he brought his hands up and framed Niall's face with them, his thumbs caressing Niall's cheekbones.

"We don't have to rush things. You barely slept last night, and you've had a lot thrown at you today," Ethan said, his thumbs continuing their soothing pattern.

Niall rocked forward, ignoring the twinge of pain in his wrist as he put more pressure on his forearm to support himself. The pain medication he'd taken hadn't done more than take the edge off the ache, but his body was practically vibrating with arousal, blotting out everything else. When Ethan wrapped his arms tightly around Niall's waist and rolled them, Niall didn't even notice the way the movement jarred the newly set bone.

Bolder now, he mouthed along the tanned column of Ethan's neck, tongue flicking out to trace his Adam's apple and taste the salty skin. Ethan's stubble rasped against the soft flesh of Niall's tongue, and he traced a line upward, seeking more of the rough texture.

"Niall."

The word was barely a breath, but it was all the encouragement Niall needed. He nudged Ethan lightly with his elbow, pressing him flat on his back so he could straddle his hips. It was an awkward position since he could only support himself with one hand, but Ethan seemed to anticipate the difficulty, bringing an arm up to brace Niall and help steady him. Niall's breath caught as he felt the ridge of Ethan's arousal underneath him, a shiver running up his spine at the knowledge that Ethan wanted him as much as he wanted Ethan. Niall still felt woozy from the pain medication and the scotch, but he wanted to show Ethan how much he needed him and how glad he was Ethan was willing to make a go of things with him even after everything that had happened.

"Whoa," Ethan said, bringing one hand up to knead the back of Niall's neck soothingly. "We have plenty of time for that later. I fully intend to have my wicked way with you when we get home, but for now you need some sleep."

"I'm fine," Niall said, melting into the neck massage.

"No, you're not. But you will be. We both will be. Nolan would want us to be."

Niall usually bristled when someone told him what they thought Nolan would have wanted, since it was usually so condescending. Ethan's words were a comfort, though, and Niall was starting to believe he and Ethan being together was actually something Nolan would be pleased about.

"I loved him too, Niall. And I can't promise things will be easy between us, but I can promise Nolan will never be something that comes between us."

Niall felt emotionally wrung out and exhausted, but he couldn't remember the last time he'd felt so happy and free. Ethan was right—Nolan would love that he and Ethan had managed to find each other and fall in love. And the part of him that had felt burdened with guilt over moving on had eased the moment Ethan had acknowledged he understood part of Niall's heart was always going to belong to Nolan.

Niall released a shuddering breath, letting Ethan shift him around until he was spooned up against him on the narrow bench seat.

"Promise?"

Ethan was silent for a minute before pressing a kiss to the back of Niall's neck. "Yes. Go to sleep, love. I'll still be here when you wake up."

BRU BAKER is a freelance journalist who writes for newspapers and magazines. She knew she was destined to be a writer by the tender age of four, when she started publishing a weekly newspaper for her family. What they called nosiness she called a nose for news, and no one was surprised when she ended up with degrees in journalism and political science and started a career in journalism.

While reporting the news is her day job, fiction is Bru's true love. Most evenings you can find her curled up with a mug of tea, some fuzzy socks, and a book or her laptop. Whether it's creating her own characters or getting caught up in someone else's, there's no denying that Bru is happiest when she's engrossed in a book. She and her husband live in the Midwest with their two young children, whose antics make finding time to write difficult but never let life get boring.

Visit Bru online at http://www.bru-baker.com or follow her on Twitter at http://www.twitter.com/bru_baker. You can also email her at bru@bru-baker.com.

Also from BRU BAKER

http://www.dreamspinnerpress.com

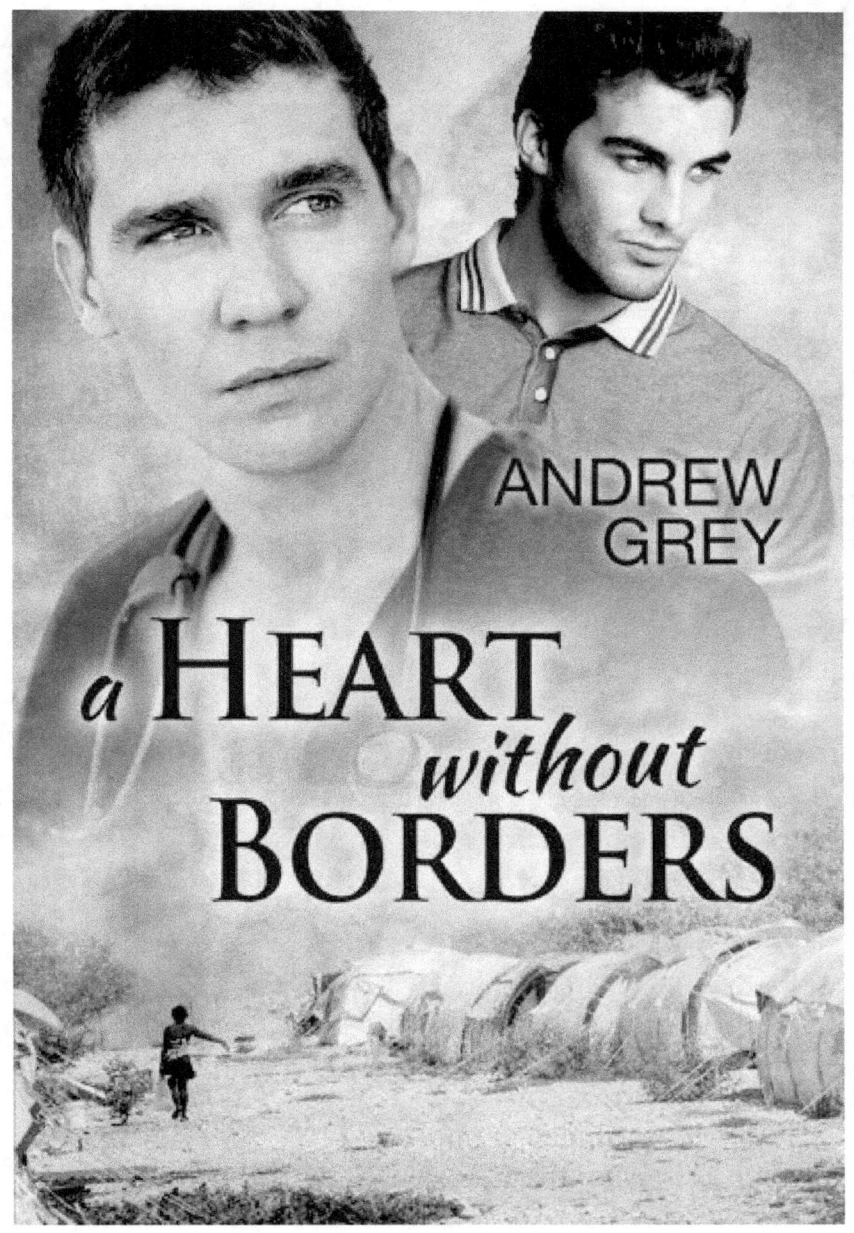